Anton *and* Cecil
Cats on Track

Also by Lisa Martin and Valerie Martin
Anton and Cecil: Cats at Sea

Anton *and* Cecil
Cats on Track

By LISA MARTIN *and*
VALERIE MARTIN

Illustrated by KELLY MURPHY

ALGONQUIN YOUNG READERS   2015

Published by
Algonquin Young Readers
an imprint of Algonquin Books of Chapel Hill
P.O. Box 2225
Chapel Hill, NC 27514-2225

a division of
Workman Publishing
225 Varick Street
New York, New York 10014

LIBRARY OF CONGRESS CATALOGING-IN-PUBLICATION DATA
Martin, Lisa, [date] author.
Anton and Cecil : cats on track / by Lisa Martin and Valerie Martin ;
illustrated by Kelly Murphy.—First edition.
pages cm
ISBN 978-1-61620-419-8
1. Cats—Juvenile fiction. 2. Brothers—Juvenile fiction. 3. Quests
(Expeditions)—Juvenile fiction. 4. Mice—Juvenile fiction. 5. Animals—Juvenile
fiction. 6. Adventure stories. [1. Cats—Fiction. 2. Brothers—Fiction. 3. Mice—
Fiction. 4. Animals—Fiction. 5. Adventure and adventurers—Fiction.]
I. Martin, Valerie, [date] author. II. Murphy, Kelly, [date] illustrator.
III. Title. IV. Title: Cats on track.
PZ7.M36354Aq 2015
813.6—dc23
[Fic]
2015004193

10 9 8 7 6 5 4 3 2 1
First Edition

For Roger, our trusted Brakeman.
And for Lorelei, our newest kit.

CONTENTS

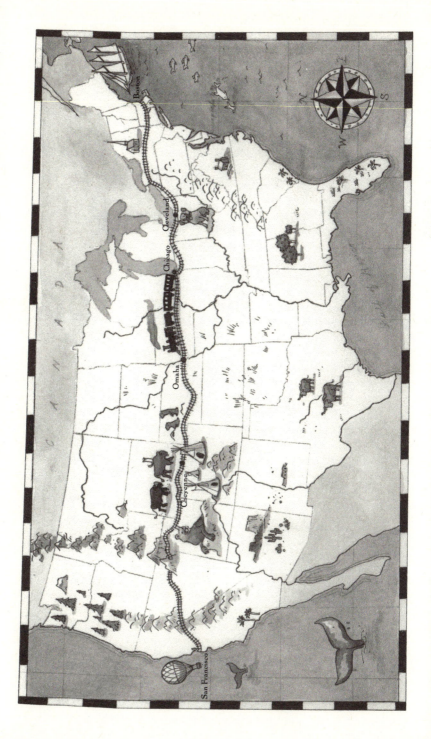

Anton *and* Cecil
Cats on Track

CHAPTER 1

The Mouse Network

A stiff breeze whooshed across the harbor at Lunenburg, setting the tall ships rocking against their moorings and snapping the flags atop the mainsail masts. Anton sat in the noonday sun next to the lighthouse, carefully cleaning his smooth gray fur. His brother Cecil sprawled next to him on the warm bricks, the white tuft on the end of his otherwise black tail flicking with amusement.

"I'm just saying, it's odd," Cecil insisted, his golden eyes twinkling. "I've never seen a lizard anywhere near as big as you've described. Are you sure it wasn't a *dog* you met on that island? A small cow, maybe?"

Anton glared briefly at Cecil and returned to his cleaning. "*Its* name was Dave, and he told me he was a lizard. So yes, I'm sure."

"Huh." Cecil rolled onto his back and stretched out his legs. "Where I come from, lizards are for eating."

"Everything's for eating where you come from," Anton said dryly.

A sudden flapping from the lighthouse path caught their attention, and Cecil rolled to his stomach. A dull white gull sailed up the path and coasted in the steady wind overhead, looking down upon the two cats with tiny, red-rimmed eyes.

"Ahoy, cats!" squawked the gull. "Is one of you called Seasick, and one Tantrum?"

"No," called Anton uncertainly, staring up at the bird. "He's Cecil, and I'm Anton."

"Close enough," said the gull, listing in the breeze. He glided lower and waved a black-tipped wing behind him. "Two mice back there, wanting to have a word with you. Say they have a message from a friend of some kind."

Cecil sat fully upright. "Mice? Two mice want to talk to us?" He grinned, showing his teeth.

Anton lifted his head, scanning the path. "I doubt it. You can't trust gulls, brother. Don't you know that yet?"

The gull rolled his eyes. "Cats," he muttered. "Suit yourselves," he called, then tilted into a U-turn on the currents of air. He flew back down the path and banked again, screeching once at a blueberry shrub on the hillside before diving swiftly away over the harbor.

Two scraggly mice, one brown and one gray, emerged from under the shrub and began making their way toward the lighthouse, dashing between rocks and tufts of grasses in little bursts.

Anton glanced at Cecil. "Now, behave, all right? Let's hear them out."

Cecil settled his girth next to Anton and licked his lips. "I always behave."

The mice stopped a short distance away and huddled together, their whiskers quivering. The brown mouse nudged the gray one, who took a breath, sat up on his hindquarters, and addressed the cats.

"We bring a message to the felines Weasel and Ant Farm from the great adventurer Hieronymus," squeaked the gray mouse solemnly.

Anton gasped. "From Hieronymus?" Anton had heard nothing of his brave mouse friend's whereabouts for many months.

"Our names are *Cecil* and *Anton*," growled Cecil. He turned to his brother. "How can they get that ridiculous mouse's name right but not ours?"

Anton shushed Cecil. "We are those cats," he said to the mice. "Go on."

The gray mouse cleared his throat. "Hieronymus sends word along the vast mouse network that he has traveled far into the land of the setting sun and now finds himself in grave danger and in need of assistance."

Anton gasped again. "What kind of danger?"

The gray mouse clutched his whiskers. "Sorry to say, he lies imprisoned in an iron fortress, guarded by a sharp-clawed dragon." The brown mouse, hunched behind the gray mouse and quivering, leaned and whispered something, and the gray mouse nodded. "And taunted by a wild-eyed witch," he added.

"How awful!" cried Anton.

Cecil smirked. "Yeah, but how reliable is this so-called mouse network?" he asked, standing and arching his back.

"Very," said the gray mouse, pulling himself up a little.

Anton began to pace. "How would we ever find him?" he asked Cecil, who shrugged and eyed the mice skeptically.

The mice leaned together, conferring. The brown mouse began shaking his head vigorously, but the gray mouse waved a paw and squeaked quietly to him. "I know, but the ship is the only way." He turned to Anton. "Our ship returns to a large port," the gray mouse explained. "We sail the day after tomorrow, and you could make the trip with us to set off in the right direction. After that, you would have to board one of the great landships to find him."

"Landships?" said Cecil. "Never heard of them."

The brown mouse threw his paws up in disgust, and the gray mouse twitched his nose at the black cat. "Have you ever traveled the world, Mr. Weasel?"

"It's *Cecil*, and you bet I have," grumbled Cecil, taking a step forward. The mice jumped back.

Anton put a paw on Cecil's thick shoulder. "Now, don't eat the messenger."

"I wasn't going to!" said Cecil, glancing at Anton innocently.

"You're drooling."

Cecil wiped his chin with his paw. "It's dinner-time," he said.

The cat brothers looked up again, but the mice had vanished from the path.

⁂

Late in the day, Anton sat by his lighthouse home and gazed at the ocean, worrying about his friend and wondering what to do. He had spent the afternoon teaching his little brother Clive how to catch crabs, but the kitten was easily distracted and made a poor student. All the way back to the lighthouse Clive asked questions about his big brothers, who were known throughout Lunenburg for their seagoing adventures. Not too long ago, Anton had been impressed as a ratter on a merchant ship, and Cecil had followed him onto the open ocean in another ship, hoping to find Anton and bring him home. Everyone agreed that something like a miracle had eventually brought them back to Lunenburg again. Clive vowed that he too would go out in the wide world on a sailing vessel. Anton thought he would have to talk with Cecil about the boy—he shouldn't be encouraged in his fantasies about life at sea, which had been, in Anton's memory, fraught with peril. When Cecil talked about it—bragged about it was a more accurate description—they had gone from triumph to triumph and never missed a meal. Anton couldn't deny that there had been good times, good food, the sailors singing the shanties he enjoyed, and the beauty of a calm sea at night. But he also remembered being hauled aboard ship by the scruff of his neck and thrown into the dark hold. He'd battled a vicious rat, been stranded on an island and attacked by huge birds, and had nearly died of starvation and thirst on an abandoned ship. That was when he'd met Hieronymus, the bold, talkative, resourceful mouse who saved both their lives by gnawing through a water barrel.

It was good to be home, and it would be fine with Anton if he never left again. Home was the same, but he knew himself to be different. One of the things he'd learned was that true friendship could be found in unexpected places. Cecil put up with Hieronymus because he knew his brother owed his life to the mouse, but Anton's regard for Hieronymus went beyond duty. Anton had come to admire and respect the mouse, though sometimes he had wished Hieronymus didn't talk quite so much. As Anton sat in the warm breeze, gazing out to sea, he recalled his last conversation with Hieronymus.

They had spoken the previous fall on a cold, clear night with a sliver of a moon and a glittering net of stars cast wide over the water. As Anton had paused at the sight of a graceful schooner bobbing lightly at anchor in the bay, he'd heard a voice come out of the air.

"You know what we call that moon?" said the voice.

Anton started and stared into the darkness. Something small and dark moved on a rock closer to shore. Anton smiled to himself. "What are you doing down here?"

Hieronymus chuckled and scooted to a closer rock. "Same as you," he said. "Stargazing."

"Right," said Anton. "So what do you call that moon?"

"Mouse whisker."

"And what about the stars?"

"They're all laid out in mouse tales."

"Mouse tails?"

"Stories. You know. About famous heroes from long ago."

"Mouse heroes," Anton repeated. "Right."

"What do you see when you look at the stars?" Hieronymus asked.

"I wasn't really looking at the stars. I was looking at that schooner and thinking of how everything here is the same as it was when we left."

"It *is* the same," said Hieronymus. "But I'm not. That's why I'm thinking of moving on."

"You're going back to sea?"

"I'm thinking of getting as far from the sea as I can. I've had a message from a cousin that I didn't know I had. His name is Eponymus. We're about the same age. While you and I were tossing about on the bounding main, he set off and wound up in a fine place. He says there aren't many cats there—excuse me, but present company excluded, that's a plus for a mouse—and he lives in a nice house. There's plenty to eat and it's quiet. I like the sound of that."

"You're looking for a quiet place?"

"I'm getting old. I don't have family here. The

young mice around now are a rough bunch and they don't have any respect for their elders. They think I'm just some old blowhard who talks too much."

"How will you find your cousin?"

"I don't know, but the lads who brought me the message said the mouse network is pretty reliable. I'll follow them."

"The mouse network," Anton had said, his eyes widening.

And now here it was. Hieronymus had sent a message through the mouse network, calling for help. Cecil wanted to pretend it was nonsense or an exaggeration, but Anton felt his friend's call should be taken seriously. Hieronymus had saved Anton's life and Anton could never forget that. Though the mouse was given to tall tales, Anton knew Hieronymus was too proud to ask for help if he didn't really need it. *I just hope this network is as good as he said it is,* Anton thought. But how was he ever going to persuade Cecil to take advice from a pair of sniveling, terrified rodents?

❖ ❖ ❖

Just after dawn, sailors and dockworkers stood on the piers and along the shoreline, frowning out at the mouth of the harbor as if waiting for a storm, or for other bad news to arrive on the breeze. Cecil and old Billy, the harbormaster's cat, sat side by side on the rocks next to Billy's house.

"Something's up," said Cecil, peering around at the men's faces. "They're acting like someone died."

"Perhaps more than one someone," said Billy, lifting his chin toward the harbor as a slow procession came into view.

Cecil squinted at the two vessels moving in a line toward the docks, bound together from stern to bow with lengths of rope. The lead boat was small with neither sails nor oars, of a type the cats called a "rumbly boat" because of the sound it made, chugging steadily through the waves. Behind it, pulled along like a rudderless toy, was a large brig, crumpled and splintered. The brig should have had four tall masts with three or more sails wrapped on the crossbars of each, but the mainmast and mizzenmast in the center had been twisted and ripped away, and the two smaller masts at the bow and stern leaned at odd angles like bent straws. Railing spokes had been pulled out like the missing teeth of pirates, and the long, thin bowsprit, usually pointing the way forward, was cracked in the middle and hung limply toward the water below. Only the winged feet of a former figurehead were visible.

"Ugh, what a sight," said Cecil.

"Mmm," agreed Billy. "One does hear of these shipwrecks from time to time. Storms, rocks, poor sailing—the traveling creatures I meet tell me that many have been lost to a watery grave."

The sight brought to Cecil's mind the ship he'd stowed away on to follow Anton after his brother had been catnapped from the docks. Dismasted in a fierce storm, that ship became a floating prison, and the only thing that had saved Cecil was an audacious escape to a marauding pirate ship.

Cecil's whiskers quivered with the memories. "Shipwrecks aren't *that* common, are they?" he asked.

"It only takes one, my lad," said Billy gravely.

"Just one to change your life," Cecil agreed.

"Are you really thinking of going out again?" Billy asked, the tip of his tail flicking nervously. The story of the rodent messengers had spread and was the talk of the cats around town, all waiting to see if the brothers were brave enough, or fool-hardy enough, to follow them.

Cecil passed a paw over one ear. "I know, it's crazy," he sighed. "We're supposed to take the word of a couple of *mice,* and shove off to rescue another *mouse* who got himself in a tight spot, without the first idea how to find him." He shook his head. "It's nuts. I don't even know where to begin."

Billy cleared his throat and hoisted his bulk to lumber down the dock. "This way," he called. Cecil followed, carefully avoiding sailor boots as he went.

"Here she is," said Billy, stopping in front of a tall clipper. "The ship the mice speak of. The Master calls her the *Sea Song.* Regular arrivals here every seven or eight days, bearing loads of metal, tools and such. From where she sails, or to where, I cannot tell you." He sat and nibbled one of his front claws thoughtfully.

Cecil let out a slow breath. He'd seen this ship before from a distance, dancing into the harbor, quick and nimble at half-sail. He looked up at the figurehead. It was a lady with long dark hair and a fish's tail instead of legs—Billy had told him she was called a "mermaid"—her mouth open as if she were singing. *Where does it go from here?* wondered Cecil, his heart beating a little faster. *A mysterious land.* He surveyed the deck, recalling his own tall ship exploits, not so long ago. Since then, the day-trips on the fishing schooners had seemed less exciting somehow.

"It's risky, you know," said Billy, watching Cecil sidelong. "Just to save a mouse. It might not be worth it."

Cecil glanced at the wreck and then up at the *Sea Song.* The ship looked strong and powerful. And fast. He swished his tail back and forth.

"Oh, I seriously doubt we'd ever find the mouse," he said, waving a paw. "And I know Anton. He's not fond of seagoing and he won't want to leave home again." He began to pace. "But it'd be fun to travel, wouldn't it?" His whiskers began to tingle with the thought of a quest. "I can't believe I'm saying this, but I think I'll try to convince him to go."

Billy turned to him somberly. "You sure, lad? You could end up on the other side of the world."

Cecil looked again at the sleek ship, long and narrow, with sail after reefed sail ready to spill wide and catch the wind, and he grinned. "Bill, old friend, that might not be so bad."

CHAPTER 2

Aboard the *Sea Song*

Anton had always enjoyed salooning, as his brother called it, but now that he had heard the sailors sing along with the accordion under the stars with the ship running fast beneath them, listening to the shanties in a crowded, smoky room was not the same. Still, it was better than nothing, so he slipped behind the customary loose wallboard and settled himself on his barrel behind the door. A glow warmed his chest as the patrons' chatter subsided and a tall, young sailor stood up to lead the singing. Anton knew for once, or thought he did, what the chatter was about. The wrecked ship hauled in that morning was the talk of the town. Humans and cats and probably even the mice had found it a sad and unnerving sight. Anton hadn't seen it yet, but Billy had told him about it when he stopped to chat with him earlier.

"When you see something like that, you know you and your brother were the lucky ones," Billy said, and this struck Anton as true. To have been stranded on one ship and then rescued by another that happened across them on the great, wide ocean was lucky indeed.

But there were many kinds of luck. Theirs had felt sometimes like a special sort, the kind that might not be wise to push. Anton tried to enjoy the singing, but his mind kept returning to the message from Hieronymus and the shipwreck, arriving so close together. It felt like a sign, but a sign of what, he couldn't guess.

The singing gave way to an argument between two bearded sailors. Anton slipped out of the saloon and headed home to the lighthouse. After a nap, he decided to have a look at the wrecked ship. As the early morning light brightened the sky, Anton rounded the quay and spotted Billy, Cecil, and that silly kitten Clive, who idolized Cecil, lounging in the shelter of the harbormaster's doorway, where they could survey the wharf without being seen.

"Has the lad been out here all night?" Anton asked Cecil as he approached.

"He's better out here in the fresh air than where you've been keeping yourself," replied Cecil. "I can smell the saloon on your coat."

"It wasn't so great in there," Anton agreed. "I thought I'd have a look at this wreck everyone's so agog about."

Billy pulled himself up with his customary huff. "It's a cautionary sight," he warned. "There was not even a mouse survived on her."

"Don't scare him," Cecil said to Billy. "He's got enough caution already."

As they ambled down the wharf to the storm-battered wreck, Anton considered Cecil's remark. It irked him, as he was well capable of taking risks if there was a good reason. Hieronymus was a good enough reason, though he was sure Cecil would disagree.

The three cats stood gazing at the broken spars, the smashed bowsprit, and the tattered bits of sail hanging from the yardarm. "Not even a mouse,"

Anton repeated. Then, as the sun pushed up over the horizon and cast a golden sheen across the deck of the ruined ship, the brothers both glimpsed a slight movement and burst into laughter. A solitary little mouse came running shakily down the line from the ship. With a wild leap, he skittered past them toward the shelter of the warehouses. As he passed, Cecil put out a paw and took in a breath, but Anton chided him. "Let him go. He's the sole survivor."

Cecil chuckled. "Probably the last of his clan."

The brothers leaned toward each other and bumped shoulders. That was how Hieronymus described himself—the last of his clan—and Anton hoped Cecil was remembering, as he himself was, how after losing his entire family the mouse had saved Anton's life by slowly, tirelessly chewing through a water barrel on a derelict ship.

"Shall we go find him?" Cecil asked.

"I wish we had more to go on."

"We'll be the first cats in history taking travel tips from rodents."

"But you're willing?" Anton asked.

Cecil shrugged. "I'm curious about these land-ships. But I didn't think you'd want to leave again."

"I don't," Anton said. "I just feel obligated. I don't think Hieronymus would send for us if he weren't in real trouble. We'll stick together this time, right?"

"As long as I'm the leader," Cecil agreed.

"I'll be the brains and you can be the brawn," Anton replied.

"Our mission is as good as accomplished," Cecil declared. "Let's go tell those silly mice we're booking passage." The brothers sauntered down the dock to have a look at the *Sea Song* and plot the best strategy for getting aboard.

※　※　※

Anton wondered how their mother Sonya would take the news. He hadn't gotten the chance to say goodbye last time, when he was impressed right off the docks in the daylight. As he and Cecil explained everything to her that morning outside the lighthouse, she was surprisingly calm.

"I'm proud of you for going to help your friend," said Sonya, nodding. She looked from Anton to Cecil, smiling slightly, then stepped in close and touched noses with each of them. "Be careful."

Three of the kittens, Clive among them, barreled out of the lighthouse, squealing and tussling. Clive spied Cecil and leaped onto his back, trying to wrestle him down, but Cecil stood sturdily and laughed. Clive slid off and sat between Cecil's front feet.

"Your brothers are going on a trip," said Sonya to the kittens, who immediately fixed their big eyes on Anton and Cecil.

"Can I come with you?" asked Clive, looking up at Cecil's white whiskers.

"No, it's too dan—" Cecil paused, as Sonya sent him a warning look. "We'll take you along when you're older."

"Will you bring us back some stories?" asked another of the kittens.

"Of course we will!" Cecil boomed. "What's an adventure without lots of good stories?"

Anton swallowed and looked at Sonya as the kittens cheered. She smiled, and winked at him.

Billy appeared on the path, puffing toward them. "It's time," he said.

❖ ❖ ❖

Cecil and Anton crouched on the hard packed dirt between two fat barrels, waiting for the right moment. Sailors grunted as they lugged the last of the cargo up the gangplank and onto the *Sea Song*, while others shimmied up the lines to loosen the sails. The cats knew what that meant: she was about to cast off, and they needed to move. Cecil could see someone with a large and elaborate hat, probably the captain, perusing a bundle of papers at the stern. Another man, very thin and wearing a bright green scarf, stood directing the crew as they reached the top of the plank with their loads. A loose plan formulated in Cecil's mind, and he raised a paw toward the thin man.

"He'll be an easy one," said Cecil. "He'll probably be pleased to see us. Everyone likes a cat or two on board, right?" He stood and stepped out from between the barrels. "Come on!"

The brothers moved with quick feet through the bustle on the dock and paused, side by side, at the bottom of the gangplank.

"Volunteering for duty!" Cecil meowed, and they began to climb up.

The thin man whirled toward the two cats and froze, an expression of horror on his face. He squinted, pulled the folds of his green scarf up over his nose, and began shaking his head rapidly. He stepped onto the plank, holding one hand up in front of him like a shield.

"He doesn't look pleased," said Anton, slowing a little.

"Follow my lead," said Cecil. "We'll win him over." He hurried toward the thin man's legs and rubbed against them affectionately, but the man shrieked and leaped away. Snatching up a broom from the deck, the man dropped the scarf from his nose and sneezed three times.

"What's he doing?" Anton asked, ducking behind Cecil.

"I don't . . ." Cecil sprang backward as the thin man swung the broom at his head. "Hey!"

The thin man sneezed again and pulled a handkerchief from his pocket to blow his nose, still aiming the broom at Cecil like a sword. The men high above in the ratlines hooted down at the scene, laughing. "The poor mate," one of them shouted. "Allergic to everything but the sea!"

"I think he's got a cold," said Anton.

"Well, that's not *our* fault." Cecil retreated a few steps and looked down. The dark seawater eddied far below the plank. If either of them fell . . . best not to think of that. "Now I see why the mice are so at home on this ship—no cats."

"We can't get past him," said Anton, crouching low on the plank. "Let's go back."

"We can make it. We'll just have to do this

together." Cecil eyed the mate. "Here's the plan. Next time he sneezes, you slip past."

"Me?" Anton squeaked. "Why me?"

"Because you're slimmer. Once you're up, make him turn around, and then I'll follow. Got it?"

"That plan is crazy. We'll both end up drowned."

Cecil glanced at Anton. "Think about Hieronymus."

Anton looked past the thin man to the deck of the *Sea Song*. "It's too far," he said.

"You can do it, Ant Farm." Cecil grinned at his brother.

The man let out an enormous sneeze, raising the broom for a moment as he did so.

"Go!" yelled Cecil.

Anton bolted under the broom and between the thin man's legs. In an instant he was through. He'd made it!

The sailor opened his eyes and dabbed at his face with the handkerchief. Cecil stood before him on the plank, swishing his tail impishly. The man blinked at Cecil and stumbled backward. Anton let out a yowl from behind. The man cried out, turning sharply. The broom fell from his hand to the water below and he lunged to the side railing for balance as Cecil dashed past. More laughter rang

out from the men on the masts as the two cats scrambled across the deck, darted into the first open hatch, and disappeared.

✧ ✧ ✧

"It's pretty dark down here," whispered Anton.

Cecil squirmed next to him and sighed. "But you can still see, right? You're a cat."

"Well, yes," Anton admitted. "Though there's not much to see, really."

The hold was only half-full, mostly crates and a few barrels. A stack of wooden boards was secured with ropes against one wall of the hold, next to the ladder to the hatch.

"I'm starving," said Cecil, his nose working. "Nothing in here smells like food, except those berries." He nodded toward some containers wrapped in burlap sacks in one corner.

"That's why we stuffed ourselves with fish before we left, remember?" said Anton.

"That was ages ago. Who knows how long this trip will take? I'm heading up." Cecil crept carefully to one end of the stack of boards and began to climb.

Anton raised his voice. "You'll be caught by that sickly mate," he called to his brother.

"Nah," said Cecil, peering up into the darkness

from the top of the stack. "It's probably nighttime now, when most of them sleep. I'll just look around for a few scraps." He tucked his front paws under his chest and settled in to wait for someone to open the hatch. When that happened, Anton knew, Cecil would dash up the ladder and blend in with the blanket of night on deck.

"That stomach of yours is nothing but trouble," muttered Anton. He closed his eyes, but he waited as well, listening along with Cecil. At last a sailor, swinging a lantern before him, threw the hatch open and climbed down to retrieve a small cask. Anton opened his eyes just long enough to glimpse Cecil slipping up and out like a shadow. *For a big guy, he's fairly quick,* Anton thought before curling into a dreamless sleep, rocked by the motion of the ship across the moonlit sea.

❖ ❖ ❖

Anton was awakened by a sound—a ripping, tearing sound nearby, followed by a slight smacking. Instantly alert, he crouched low, slinking past the crates on silent paws. *Not a rat,* he thought. *Please not a big ugly rat trapped down here with me.* He took a deep breath and peeked slowly around the crates.

On top of the burlap sacks in the corner sat

the two mice who had brought the message from Hieronymus, feasting on blueberries. Anton blew out his breath and sat down, watching them. The gray mouse reached through the hole he had clawed in the sack and pulled out a fat berry, then turned to Anton.

"We meet again," said the gray mouse, his pointed nose covered in blue juice.

"So we do," said Anton. "How long a journey is this, anyway?"

"Not long," said the gray mouse between bites. "We'll arrive at the next daylight."

The brown mouse sat stiffly atop the bag, keeping one eye on Anton as he ate. He leaned and whispered something to his sidekick that Anton did not catch.

"Right!" squeaked the gray mouse. "Almost forgot." He turned to Anton. "There was another part of the message."

"Another part?" said Anton, frowning. "Why didn't you tell us before?"

"Your friend, the big guy." The gray mouse winced. "He's got a look in his eye, that one. Too dangerous, we had to go."

"Never mind him. What's the other part?"

The gray mouse held his berry, looking mystified for a moment. He consulted with the brown mouse quietly, then sat up tall. "Got it. Ahem. Hieronymus says he's to be found 'between the whale and the coyote.'"

Anton opened his eyes wide. "Between the whale and the coyote," he repeated. "What's a coyote?"

"No idea." The mice began cleaning their faces with their tiny forearms. A thud on the deck above made them jump and they scurried away, knocking berries to the floor as they scrabbled.

The brown mouse paused to glance back at Anton. "Good luck," he squeaked softly. "You'll need it." And the mice vanished into a crack in the wall.

Anton stepped forward to nibble on a few of the strewn berries. Alone in the dark hold, he felt his heart stutter in a way it hadn't for months. *Oh, yes,* he thought. *We'll need it.*

CHAPTER 3

Shriek and Growl

It had seemed like a good idea at the time.

After all, Cecil had visited a ship's galley before. He knew it was the place where food was prepared for the crew, often haphazardly, where chunks of meat or fish might be found wedged between barrels, and drips of stew could be lapped up from the floorboards next to the stove. Perhaps part of a hard biscuit to nibble on, but that wasn't real food, in Cecil's view. The galley of the *Sea Song* was empty of humans, as he'd hoped, though a lantern still burned on the sideboard, and he found a small wedge of hard cheese and some dried peas for his snack. As he sat and cleaned his face, he could hear the clickings and scurryings of rodents in the walls. *A shame,* he thought. *A good ship's cat could whip this place into shape in no time.*

There was a stomping down the steps toward the doorway. The only problem with the galley, Cecil suddenly recalled, was that there was just one way out. He caught a quick glimpse of a sailor stepping in with an armload of tin plates, and he dashed into the tiny larder, squeezing himself behind a tall sack. The sailor dumped the plates into a wooden tub, then picked up the lantern from the sideboard and walked out again, pulling the door shut behind him.

Cecil groaned. He really should have been more careful. Now he was stuck, and Anton would worry. "Ah, well," he said to himself as he made his way through the darkness over to the tub to lick the plates clean. "It's a nice place to be stuck." A little snooze on top of the flour sack, and he'd wake up refreshed, and the crew would have to eat again sometime.

But hours passed and Cecil felt the ship slow and then stop. The thudding and banging of dockside activities began, and he paced in the galley. Were they not even going to come in to prepare that foul black liquid they drank at all hours? He positioned himself near the door and listened to the sailors tromping back and forth on the deck above. He tried to think like Anton. What would he do? Anton wouldn't venture off the ship alone, so Cecil would have to get back to the hold to find him—as soon as somebody opened this blasted door.

✤ ✤ ✤

Heavy boots tramped across the deck above Anton's head, and he could hear muffled voices shouting and answering as the steady rolling of the ship quieted. Anton guessed they were coming in to dock, but Cecil hadn't returned. The hatch hadn't been reopened, so he was still up there, somewhere. *Should I get off the ship by myself?* Anton wondered. *What if Cecil's gotten himself trapped, or captured?*

The hatch creaked open, spilling in sunlight. Anton pressed himself against a barrel as several crewmen climbed down the ladder and began hoisting crates onto their shoulders to carry up again. He slipped behind the men and crossed the hold. As quietly as he could, Anton scaled the stack of boards as Cecil had done and crouched to wait for his chance to escape.

"Aw, something got into the berries," said a sailor in the corner, holding up the torn bag with one hand. The others stopped and scanned the grimy walls for a moment as if they might spot the culprit. Anton put his face between his paws and tried to flatten himself along the boards. The sailors shrugged and bent to heave more cargo, and Anton saw his opportunity. With a running leap he sprang to the ladder and scrambled through the opening without a sound.

Out on the deck, Anton blinked in the sunlight and gasped.

Before him was a wharf, and beyond it was a city bigger and busier than Anton had ever seen or dreamed of. Horse-drawn carriages and loaded wagons crowded the street. Dogs, cats, and chickens wove among the legs of people thronging everywhere. Children laughed and ran past adults selling knives, bottles of liquid, candles, pots and pans, all manner of clothes, and food in roadside stands. Behind all of them rose tall buildings along blocks that seemed to stretch outward forever.

The noise hit Anton like a wave over the bow—the shouting and neighing and rumbling, all unceasing. The chaotic scene made the unpredictable ocean seem calm and inviting by comparison.

As Anton stood, mouth ajar, taking everything in, he heard a loud sneeze from behind him. He flinched and looked back, straight into the watery eyes of the first mate who'd blocked their way. The mate pulled the green scarf covering his nose down long enough to bellow, "Off my ship this instant!" Wielding the broom, he charged at Anton.

For a second Anton froze. Should he stay and try to find Cecil, or disembark and wait for him on land? No time to decide before the mate was upon Anton, shooing him frantically toward the gangplank. Anton dodged to one side, glancing toward the bow and then the stern for any sign of a big black ball of fur, but the mate hustled Anton down the plank at broom-point.

In the middle of the muddy roadbed, Anton sidestepped cart wheels and the boots of strangers. He swiveled his ears, listening for Cecil's voice in the crowd. He dove into the shadows behind one of the stalls and surveyed the hectic activity on the street, a knot of fear twisting in the pit of his stomach. He'd lost Cecil already and had not the first idea where to go from here.

The *Sea Song* still rested against the dock, her gangplank empty now, her sails wrapped tightly around the crossbars. Anton gazed at the ship in a panic. It was the last connection he had to anything familiar, and he felt its pull. Then Hieronymus's voice floated through his mind, and Anton remembered being trapped in a cage at an animal market on a distant island with his friend. The mouse could have escaped easily to save himself, but he refused. *I've pledged my troth!* he'd declared, holding up a paw. *I will not leave a friend in danger.* Anton shook his head sheepishly. Hieronymus would not give up so easily.

The noise of the bustling town settled around Anton, and he began to hear distinct sounds in the din. Crying children, screeching shorebirds, shouts of men's laughter, and the creak of wagon wheels. One sound he could not place. It hung heavy as a storm cloud above and below and among the others. Anton could feel its vibrations in his rib cage, but it was not the pleasing music of the saloons. This was a dense, chuffing sound, like bursts of wind against the sails, or an enormous creature taking slow, panting breaths. Anton didn't know what it was, and it terrified him.

❖ ❖ ❖

At long last the cook and the cabin boy burst into the galley, not even noticing as Cecil scampered behind their legs and up the steps to the main deck, awash in sunlight. He hustled to the hatch, which lay wide open, and peered down into the hold. His stomach lurched. The space was empty; all of the crates and barrels and even the stacks of boards had been carried out. "Anton!" Cecil's voice echoed in the hold. But he knew his brother was gone—there was nothing left to hide behind.

Cecil straightened up. What now? Only a few crewmen were about, including the sneezy mate, clutching his dastardly broom and talking with the captain down by the ship's wheel. There were lots of other places Anton could be hiding—under tarps or inside coils of rope, down in the fo'c'sle, up in the ratlines, but . . . Cecil's nose began to twitch.

What was that smell?

He turned his head slowly toward the pier, his eyes narrowing and his nose working furiously. Among the people and carts and animals crowding the roadbed, Cecil detected the scents of roasted meats, freshly baked bread, simmering stews, and an ocean of fish, all close at hand, some of it in plain sight as humans behind counters held steaming packets out to others passing by. On their own, his paws began moving toward the gangplank.

"Surely Anton would go this way," Cecil murmured, breaking into a trot at the sound of the mate shrieking behind him. "Any cat worth his salt would."

He reached the docks and continued right on, his nose in the air and leading the way. *Anton must be hungry,* Cecil reasoned. *He's had no snack. So what would he* . . . Cecil turned and sprang out of the path of a horse pulling a loaded wagon. *That was close.* He recovered his balance, then yowled as his tail was smashed under the boot of a little boy running past holding several steaming sticks above his head. Cecil bared his teeth to hiss at the boy, but noticed that he'd dropped one of the sticks, and it smelled like something with great potential. What luck! The stick ran straight through the middle of several chunks of fish. Cecil quickly clamped one end of the stick in his mouth and darted behind a tree on the far side of the roadbed.

He had just figured out how to hold the stick

down with both paws and pull the fish away with his teeth when he felt the close presence of another creature. Cecil lifted his eyes to see a small orange cat creeping toward him, low to the ground. It was just a kitten really, a male with a skinny tail and big ears, and he froze under Cecil's glare. Cecil continued gobbling down the fish and the kitten advanced smoothly, like a little hunter. Finally Cecil stepped away and began cleaning his paws, leaving a fat chunk behind on the stick. The kitten dashed forward and leaped upon the fish, wrestling off little bites while gazing up at Cecil.

"I haven't seen you before," said the kitten with his mouth full. "You just get here?"

"That's right." Cecil nodded. "Passing through."

"Where you going?" asked the kitten.

Cecil paused. "To rescue a friend, you could say."

The kitten nodded. "That's nice of you."

"Maybe," said Cecil, turning to the kitten. "Say, do you happen to know anything about landships?"

The kitten sat up, his round eyes wide, his long pink tongue licking the fish from his lips. "Landships!" He thought for a moment, then shook his head. "Nope. What are they?"

"They're the way we need to get where we're going," said Cecil, suddenly remembering Anton.

The kitten looked around. "Who's we?"

Cecil had opened his mouth to explain when a high whistle blew in the distance, followed by a deep, rasping chug, and then another, and another, slow and even. "My whiskers!" said Cecil, his ears cocked. "What is that?"

The kitten gave a tiny sigh. "That," he said, solemnly, "is something we call *rolling death*."

Cecil eyed the kitten closely. "What do you mean, rolling death? That sounds horrible!"

"It does, because it is." The kitten bobbed his little head up and down. "It's a huge carriage that moves without anything pulling it, and it's loud and ugly, and my mom says if you get too close it'll roll right over you. She says that's how Uncle George disappeared."

"A carriage that moves without anything pulling it," said Cecil softly. "This I've got to see. And it's over that way, you say?" he asked the kitten, pointing a paw.

"Well, yes, but don't go over there!" said the kitten, arching his back above his skinny legs.

"Didn't you hear the part about it squishing you, and Uncle George?"

Cecil smiled at the kitten knowingly. "What do they call you?" he asked, appraising its orange fur. "Pumpkin?"

"Herman."

"Well, Herman, I say don't be a chicken, be a cat! Get out there and have an adventure!"

Herman swiveled his ears at another blast from the whistle. He shook his head. "No thanks. Too dangerous."

"Fair enough," said Cecil, turning to leave. "But if you see my brother Anton passing through, be sure to introduce yourself. You two have a lot in common." He gave a side-to-side swish of his tail and disappeared into the crowd of legs on the roadbed.

⁓ ⁓ ⁓

Anton was overpowered by the strange chuffing sound. He backed up cautiously, drawing his head in as if to avoid a blow. A shriek like a giant hawk tore through the air in front of him at the same time as a blast of wet, hot air struck him from behind. Without thinking, he whirled about, claws out, his jaws wide to issue a warning hiss of his own. He was facing two wet, black nostrils the size of his head. Before he could figure out what he was seeing, the nostrils flew up before him and he realized it was a horse, now stretching his big head skyward, his glassy eyeballs rolling down at Anton and his hairy lips quivering.

"Whoa, whoa there," said the horse. "Don't put those claws in my nose, for neighing out loud."

Anton sheathed his claws and ran a paw over his mouth to smooth his whiskers. He'd seen horses on the docks at home, but he'd always tried to steer clear of them, as they were clearly dangerous. This was the biggest horse he'd ever seen, and the hairiest. Even his hooves were draped in a deep fringe of fur. Anton had never spoken to a horse before, but this one looked so upset he thought he'd best be polite.

"Excuse me," he said. "You took me by surprise."

"Well, that's no reason to threaten somebody with claws in the nose."

"I'm afraid that's not entirely in my control," Anton explained.

The horse worked his lips, as if thinking over this reply, gradually lowering his head. "You mean the claws just come out automatically?"

"Sometimes," Anton replied. "I can make them come out when I want to, but if I'm frightened, it's not something I think about. I just know I may need them, I guess."

"When I'm frightened, I run as fast as I can," the horse said. "And I guess I don't really think about it."

"I'll bet nobody gets in your way," Anton observed.

The horse seemed to find this amusing. "No," he said. "I'm a big guy. No human's going to catch me, running on those flimsy feet they have."

Anton took in the leather strips and wooden poles that strapped the horse to a wagon loaded with heavy-looking bags. "My name is Anton," he said.

"I'm Solitaire," the horse said. "Or that's what my mother called me. My master calls me Nutmeg. We work here, most days. Do you live around here?"

"No," Anton said. "I just got off that ship." He lifted his chin to indicate the gangplank of the *Sea Song*, from which a steady stream of men and crates now issued. "I was with my brother, but we got separated and I can't see anything in this crowd."

"What's he look like?" Solitaire asked.

"He's bigger than me, black, white whiskers, long fur."

The horse looked out over the crowd, moving his head slowly from side to side. Anton noticed something he surely knew but had never thought about before, which was that a horse couldn't look at what was in front of him because his eyes were on either side of his head. "I don't see him," Solitaire said, bringing his head down close to Anton.

Anton tried looking between pairs of legs, around long skirts, and through the wheels of Solitaire's wagon. "I don't know how I'm going to find him."

"You want to get up on my back?" the horse suggested.

Anton was surprised. He looked up at Solitaire's wide back. The view from there would undoubtedly be worth having, but even at a run, he wasn't sure he could make the leap. "I don't think I can jump that high," he said.

"Well if you can sheathe those claws, I'll put my head down and you can walk up my neck. You can hold on to my mane if you need to—that won't hurt me."

Anton studied the horse. It was definitely doable. "That would be very kind of you," he said.

Solitaire lifted his upper lip and forced out a startling blast of warm moist air from his nostrils. "You're a polite little creature," he said. "I like that." Then he lowered his head until his mouth nearly touched the ground. "Jump on," he said.

Anton, conscious of his claws with every step, dashed up Solitaire's neck, past his shoulders to his wide, flat back. There Anton sat, curling his tail around him. It was amazing, comfortable and roomy—there was space to stretch out and take a nap up there. The horse's fur was smooth and had a pleasant scent, something Anton never would have expected. And he could see clear across the wharf. "Wow," he said. "This is great. I can see everything."

Solitaire swerved his neck around so that he could see his new passenger. "It must be hard to be so small," he said. "You never get a view."

Anton looked this way and that, trying to spot a black cat with a white paintbrush tail, but there was too much activity to focus on one spot for long. Nearby was a line of booths where people crowded, many carrying baskets laden with food. Anton thought that might be a likely spot to look for his brother.

Solitaire followed his gaze. "That's a good place;

humans go there and get all kinds of stuff to eat. My master goes there most days and sometimes he gets me an apple. I really like those."

As Anton watched the milling crowd, he spotted a child standing next to a basket and behind a woman who was talking with one of the vendors in the stalls. The child was pointing at him and calling out something he couldn't hear, but the mother did, and turned to see what was wrong. She glanced up at Anton—a cat on a horse, yes, that was amusing—and then resumed her conversation as the child continued to point and crow joyfully. Then . . . *But no. It couldn't be!*

Anton recognized the toddler: it was the baby from that ship, the one on which he'd met Hieronymus, and on which they had both nearly starved. The child's mother was the kind woman who had made a bed for Anton. One strange morning, he and Hieronymus had awakened to find that mother and child—and all the other passengers on their ship— had disappeared, leaving Anton and Hieronymus alone and adrift until their miraculous rescue. But here they were, mother and child, safe and sound in a busy town, and the baby recognized him. This comforted Anton, but it reminded him of his own mission to get to Hieronymus.

Anton shifted his paws and looked out in the other direction. In the distance he could see a long roofline and before it clouds of white smoke, but a small building in between blocked his view. Then he heard it again, that loud chugging sound, and after that—so unexpected and loud that he stood up on all fours, ready to leap to the ground—a shrill whistle tore the air.

"What's that?" Anton exclaimed.

"Calm down," the horse advised him. "It's the horseless carts. That whistle means they're about to start moving."

"Where do they go?"

"I'm hobbled if I know. But the bigger question is *how* do they go. They just make a lot of noise and of course they have wheels—you've got to have wheels—but nothing pulls them as far as I can see. And they're dangerous."

"Are they ships?"

Solitaire raised a hoof and pulled his head forward so that the straps grew tight on his neck, making a snuffling sound with his nose. "Ships," he said. "No, they're not ships. Ships go on water. These go on land."

"Landships," Anton concluded.

"That's good. You could call them that."

"It's what the mice call them," Anton said.

"Mice!" Solitaire raised his head and cast a wild eye at Anton. "One thing I don't like is mice. They scare the hooves off of me."

Anton smiled at the idea of an animal Solitaire's size being afraid of a mouse, but he didn't say anything, because he felt certain the horse had just set him on the track to find his brother.

"Try talking to the mice," Anton said. "Sometimes they understand."

He took another long look around, back toward the ship—he could see the sailors pulling in the plank—then across the wharf to the food stalls—the baby and mother had moved on, no cats were in sight—and then along the buildings that stood between the wharf and that thick column of white smoke. "Cecil will go to the landships. He may be there already."

"I take it you're coming down," said Solitaire.

"I am," he said. "I can't thank you enough."

The horse lowered his head and Anton descended in two bounds. "I hope you find your brother," the horse said.

Anton nodded. "I'll be a sad cat if I don't."

The horse brought his big head down close and touched Anton's back with his warm nose. "Good luck to you."

"Goodbye," Anton said, and he dashed across the dirt road to the shelter of another wagon parked alongside a shed. When he looked back he saw the horse standing, one hoof cocked and his long neck relaxed, his eyes closed, waiting patiently for his master to come back. Anton wondered about Solitaire's life. *He seems content enough, though he can't go anywhere without his cart. I hope his master buys him an apple.* And then he heard another shriek from the landship and took off in the direction of the sound.

CHAPTER 4

The Owl and the Pussycats

Though his brother probably would not willingly go see anything referred to as "rolling death," Cecil was terribly curious. He told himself that he'd just take a peek, then he'd hightail it back to the wharf to find Anton and get on with the business of rescuing the mouse. Avoiding boots and cart wheels, he dashed from one safe spot to the next down a long block and around two corners. He followed the sounds of rib-rattling chugs and clanging bells that carried over the mixed-up din of human chatter. At last, at the end of a dusty street lined with buildings that stretched as high as the tallest ship's mast he'd ever seen, Cecil stepped into a large town square and gazed at the commotion.

Horses clopped across the square dragging open carriages, the drivers flicking long whips over their flanks as passengers talked and laughed inside. It seemed that everywhere Cecil looked, one or another man in a long coat and high hat hurried past, often accompanied by a lady wearing a flowered or feathered hat, trying to hold the hand of a mischievous child or two. Other men lugged boxes on their shoulders to and from carts, or leaned against lampposts holding newspapers in front of their faces. From a protected spot by the glass front of a shop, Cecil tried to see through the mass of legs and carriage wheels, but all he could make out of interest were several rows of straight, thick strips of metal embedded in the pavement of the square, extending out of sight in both directions. People crossed over them without looking down, as if they were of no consequence.

"Kitty!" cried a little girl wearing a bright yellow dress, white gloves, and shiny black shoes. She held her hand out to Cecil, who sniffed obligingly. The girl smiled at him but was quickly pulled away by her mother and hustled down the street.

A filthy brown dog brushed past at a trot. "Out of my way, feline."

"Hey!" called Cecil after him. "Which way to the . . . rolling death?"

The dog's floppy ears lifted and he stopped to look back at Cecil doubtfully. "The what?"

"The . . . thing that's making all that noise." Cecil lifted his chin to the thunderous sound filling the air. It seemed to be coming from everywhere, echoing off the buildings and windows, accompanied by sharp smells that he couldn't place.

The dog let out a chuckling woof and rolled his eyes. "The *growler*, you mean. It's right over there, you can't miss it." He jerked his head toward the far end of the square and trotted away. Cecil could hear him muttering as he went. "Cats. Always their heads in the clouds."

Cecil hurried down the street, sticking close to the shop walls and ducking past doorways until he reached the end of the sidewalk. He crouched under a bench and looked out. There on the edge of the square was an enormous structure, as wide as four or five buildings set side by side and enclosed by a giant curved roof. Both ends of the structure were open so it resembled a broad tunnel, and arches composed of crisscrossed rods stretched along the ceiling like immense spiderwebs.

But the thing that captured Cecil's attention was the contraption that protruded halfway out of the near end of the structure. It stood, gleaming and muscular, chuffing like an impatient draft horse. It was long and rounded, as if the lighthouse at Lunenburg had been turned on its side and set upon huge cart wheels. Cecil was astonished that a thing that size—not nearly as big as a ship—could make that much noise. The shrill whistle made him squeeze his eyes shut, and he could feel the deep rumbling down to the pads of his paws. Thick gray clouds rose from the top of the "growler," as the dog had called it, while men climbed up into the back and called down to others from open windows. The area farthest forward near the ground was pointed, like an upside-down prow of a ship.

Oh, cat's whiskers, Cecil thought, and sighed. *I hate to leave, but I'd really better find Anton.* He stood to make his way back to the docks. But just then, the growler began to move.

❖ ❖ ❖

Anton left the wharf behind, hardly noticing the bustle around him. He passed close to buildings that grew taller and taller, as if they had been stacked one on top of the other. He rounded one corner and then another, guessing now, because he couldn't hear anything over the noise of the traffic in the street. He reached the end of a big stone building and found himself before a wide, dusty road. There a muddle of carriages and carts loaded with humans and all manner of boxes moved briskly toward an enormous open building with two entrances the size of barns. A huge, black, smoke-belching monster of a machine hissed and steamed halfway out of one of these, while men hurried back and forth across the raised metal strips that stretched out in different directions, glittering in the dirt.

Is that it? Anton wondered. He paused, taking in the scene. His first impression of the landship was that it was impenetrable and somehow cruel-looking, unlike the great sailing ships even a cat couldn't help but admire. There was nary a sail in sight.

Anton pressed against the wall of the last building, looking for a place to hide. Across a narrow cobbled alley and extending into the open-sided building was a wide raised platform on which humans milled about, carrying bundles and baskets. There were a few stalls and some tables set out with long benches, where families were occupied unwrapping parcels and distributing the contents to one another. They were laughing and talking and eating. *EATING!* When was the last time Anton had eaten? Too long. Also, a place where humans were eating might be a likely destination for his brother. Anton streaked across the alley and bounded up the steps to the platform.

Appetizing smells greeted him, and none of the humans took much notice, so he crept along the benches, his eyes, ears, and nose on high alert. A family repacking their basket at the nearest table dropped something that smelled like the cooked meat humans liked to eat onto the dusty wooden floor. One of the children stooped to pick it up, but the father reprimanded him, and he pulled his hand away, turning to join the group as they strode toward the far end of the platform. Anton darted and pounced all in one burst, and then he ran, the discarded morsel clamped in his jaws, back down the steps and beneath them where it was safe and dark. It was a tasty bit of meat, still attached to a bird-like bone, and with a little effort he was able to pry every last greasy bit away. He spent a few pleasant moments licking his lips and cleaning his whiskers. Anton wasn't adventuresome, but he sometimes felt pleased with the resourcefulness that adventure brought out in him. Travel made him more observant, focused, and quick-witted, unlike Cecil, who muscled his way through the world. *Cecil,* Anton thought. *And where in this great world is he?*

Anton crept to the edge of his shelter and looked out. As he did the landship shrieked and a horrific sound of grinding metal tore through the air, a combination that caused him to flatten to the ground, squeezing his eyes shut. After a moment he raised his haunches, prepared to back into the farthest corner of the stairwell, but first he opened his eyes and searched the crowded street once more.

And there, sidestepping wheels and hooves and perambulating humans with unusual speed and grace, was Cecil. Anton stuck his head out and yowled, "I'm here!" Somehow his brother heard his call, changed direction, ducked under a stationary cart, bounded across the set of metal strips in the ground, skirted one of the monstrous machines that had begun to crawl out of the building, and with a final triumphant leap, landed at the foot of the staircase.

"Brother," Cecil said, "this is the place!"

"I know," Anton replied smoothly. "That big monster making all the racket over there . . ." He paused and they both gazed at the steaming, chuffing machine that was now pulling out of the shelter, its great iron wheels grinding as humans and animals scattered before it.

Then the brothers spoke as one. "*That's* a landship."

❖ ❖ ❖

A bright white moon rose in the night sky and settled among the stars, and Anton tracked its path, watching from his hiding place. He sometimes took comfort in the moon's light as it passed over the land like a great cat's eye, but he was distracted now, waiting. He wanted to do something, anything, to get this rescue mission underway. All but a few of the men had gone from the immense, high-ceilinged building, and the loud, smoke-belching contraptions were dark and still. Wedged against a cold wall just inside the building's cavernous doorway, Anton and Cecil waited behind several large trunks for some clue as to what to do next with these mystifying landships.

"Well, look," said Cecil, clawing halfway up to rest his chin on his forepaws on the top of the trunk. "If it's anything like a *sea* ship, then we have to get aboard before she sails."

"Agreed," whispered Anton. "But how?" He raised his head just enough to see over, his green eyes glowing in the moonlight. "There's no gang-plank. And which one do we choose?" Behind the fearsome lead ship stood many others, each with its own set of wheels, all similar in size but without the stubby mast and the pointed prow of the carriage at the front.

"I don't know, but that lead one seems to be in charge," said Cecil.

"I'd prefer a quieter one." Anton lifted his nose a bit to sniff the night air. So many strange smells, but there was something familiar on the breeze, something sharp and bitter.

Cecil pulled himself to the top of the trunk and pricked up his ears. "I hear something—a snack maybe. Be right back." And the white tip of his fluffy black tail disappeared over the other side.

"Cecil," Anton hissed. "You shouldn't . . ." He paused and sniffed. There it was again. A pungent, acrid scent, wafting in from somewhere very near. He raised his head a little more and peered down the length of the open building, but he couldn't see anything moving besides his brother, slinking low across the gray streaks in the road, heading for the hulking, silent landships.

Anton held his body perfectly still and swiveled his ears, trying to focus on the smell, unpleasant yet vaguely known to him, like the memory of a bad dream. He heard a soft rush, a slight rustle that could have been the wind through the trees or the swish of a lady's dress. Anton cocked his head and, with a sudden chill in his bones, recognized the hush of feathered wings, bearing steeply down in flight, straight toward his brother.

Anton sprang up. "Cecil!" he shrieked. "Behind you! Duck!"

Cecil flinched and whipped around to see the enormous talons of a great dark bird closing in on him like a storm from the sky. He leaped forward, his claws skidding on the dusty pavement as he scrambled to gain traction. The bird arched its wide wings and reached its talons for Cecil's tail, not slowing a bit. Cecil veered sharply toward the only cover he could reach in time—the blackness of the space underneath the landship. The bird's claws closed and missed, and Cecil disappeared.

The bird swiftly angled its wings and pulled up, gliding past and circling back, then alighted on a rail on top of the landship just above Cecil's hiding place. With eyes like round yellow moons, it glared hard in Anton's direction. Anton flattened himself against the ground between the wall and the trunk, his chest thumping. The bird was an owl, he knew, though a bigger one than he'd ever seen and probably almost as good as a cat at seeing in the dark. When he ventured a look over the trunk again, he saw his brother's white whiskers glowing in the moonlight, the owl directly above.

"Heads up!" he shouted to Cecil.

Cecil looked up quickly and retreated under the ship. He was probably safe there, Anton thought, if he just stayed put. Even a big bird wouldn't want to fight a cat in a tight space with no room to fly.

The owl folded its wings and looked around in a slow arc as if settling in for a siege. Many minutes passed with the three of them pinned in place, until finally Anton couldn't stand the suspense any longer. He had to get closer to Cecil. He scouted a few points of shelter in the yard, took a deep breath, and eased out from behind the trunk. Slinking flat to the ground, he crept silently toward Cecil's hiding spot and pressed himself under a large water tank.

The owl swung its stout head smoothly around to gaze at Anton. In the moonlight Anton could see tufts of feathers sticking up on top, like pointed ears or horns. Its long hooked beak protruded in a dark slash just under its eyes. Brown and black feathers circled the yellow eyes in such a way that they seemed to take up half of its head.

"Ah, the cowardly savior emerges," the owl said, its voice deep and hollow like wind through tall pines. "If not for you, I'd be enjoying a tasty meal right now."

"Oh, you think so, do you?" called Cecil from the shadows below. "Well come and get me, then."

"Perhaps you don't realize to whom you are issuing this reckless challenge," the owl said. "I am a great horned owl, one of the finest predators in the avian kingdom."

"You'll be one step closer to extinction if you stick your beak under this carriage," Cecil retorted.

Anton thought fast. Cecil was making things worse. This bird was no seagull—this bird was intelligent and vain.

"Don't you know the old song?" Anton said calmly to the owl.

The bird swiveled its head to Anton. "What song?"

Anton raised his voice so his brother could hear.

> "A cat one night while on the prowl
> was dinner for a great horned owl.
> Before the night had turned to day,
> the great horned owl had passed away."

The owl tightened its talons on the railing. "Are you implying that cats are poisonous to owls?"

"Yes," called Cecil from under the carriage. "Fatal. Everyone knows that."

Anton watched the big owl yawn and shake out its wings, considering the possibilities.

"Excuse me, great horned owl," Anton began, but the owl interrupted.

"Athena is my name." The owl shifted position, her talons pinging lightly on the rail.

Anton cleared his throat and spoke up. "Athena, then. Do you know how these landships work?"

Athena blinked at him. "Landships," she repeated. "I don't know what you mean."

Anton sighed. "The thing you're sitting on," he
said, enunciating. "Isn't that a landship?"

Athena blinked again, her expression still stern.
"It is not. Some birds call it a *screecher*, as it pro-
duces an admirable screech before it moves, louder
than even our most piercing cries." She demon-
strated by lifting her head and producing an earsplitting scream, which made Anton shudder. "But
the humans made it, and they call it a *train*," she
added. "They shout the word all day long."

"Train," Anton repeated. This owl was a know-
it-all; perhaps Anton could keep her talking until
she'd forgotten about her planned meal. "Do the
trains travel into the setting sun?"

The owl turned her head impossibly far around
and looked down the path of thick gray metal
strips embedded in the pavement. "Often they do,"
she said, "though just as often they come from that
direction instead."

Cecil's voice floated up from his place in the
shadows. "How do you know which one to get on?"

Athena returned her gaze to Anton. "I've been
told that cats are more intelligent than dogs. Myself,

I doubt it. What creature in its right mind would want to *get on* a train? Animals don't travel with humans unless they're in a cage."

"We have a mission," Anton replied. He didn't think the owl would sympathize with a mission to rescue a mouse, so he left it at that.

But Cecil had to have the last word with the owl. "I bet we've traveled farther than you have. We've crossed the ocean on ships, and not in a cage, either. We may not have wings, but we know how to get where we're going."

Athena paused and clacked her beak, deliberating. The sound set Anton's teeth on edge and he waited in silence. Finally she raised one long wing with a flourish. Anton tensed, but she was merely pointing. "It's quite straightforward," she said. "All of these carriages lined up *here* are connected to, and pulled by, the train in the first position *there*. That's called the engine."

"Engine," Anton repeated. "Right."

"The engine follows the *track* in the ground. It travels only on the track, never away from it."

Anton nodded, and Athena swept the other wing into the air pointing the opposite way. "You can choose any of the carriages to *get on,* but I'd avoid those with lots of humans if I were you." She eyed Anton. "Which I am very glad that I am not."

"Which are the ones with fewer humans?" asked Anton.

Athena fluffed her wings impatiently. "At the far end the carriages are hollow, like boxes, with doors that slide open and closed." She paused again, rotating her head as she inspected the length of the train, then continued in a softer tone. "You know, you really shouldn't wait until the sun rises, because all of the humans will come back and they'll chase you away." She raised her voice a little, leaning over the side so Cecil could clearly hear. "I advise you to go *now,* to be safe."

A long silence stretched across the yard as the cats considered this advice.

"Anton?" called Cecil from underneath. His moonlit whiskers protruded from the dark space next to the wheel, and the owl seemed to swell a bit, watching from above.

"Right here," Anton replied.

"Does she look hungry to you?"

Anton heard the warning in Cecil's voice. "Oh yes, brother. She looks hungry to me."

"Brothers?" said Athena with delight. "How sweet." She was poised to dive now.

"Cats are sweet," said Cecil. "But not to eat."

"We shall see about that," said Athena. She perched, motionless as any good hunter, holding both cats in her sights and waiting for their slightest mistake.

The minutes crept past. Anton tried to think. If he moved from under the tank, he'd be exposed. Cecil could stay under his train, but Anton saw that large snarls of metal parts hung down where each carriage connected to the next, so moving quickly underneath them in either direction would be difficult. And the owl was right—if they stayed where they were until morning, the humans might not let them board. He didn't know if trains had rodent problems.

Anton suspected Athena could wait all night. He wondered if Cecil had any bright ideas.

And then they all heard it—a scuffling sound near a tall stack of papers bound with string on the ground near the engine. Anton saw the owl's eyes lift, her head flick toward the noise. Cecil's whiskers rose and turned in the shadows as well. A fat rat crept out from behind the stack and sat up, nibbling intently on a seed, oblivious to the three pairs of eyes upon it.

With barely a ruffle, Athena dropped from her perch and swooped down toward the rat. Cecil's head poked out as he watched the owl's silent descent, and Anton realized that this was their chance.

"Cecil! Run!" Anton bounded from under the tank and scampered across the yard, swerving away from the engine when he reached Cecil's spot. "Come on!" he shouted, but Cecil had already shot from the dark hiding place and into step with him. They sprinted down the length of the building in a narrow corridor between two sets of linked train carriages, dodging boxes and bags, the strong smells of metal and machinery in their noses. As they raced, Anton tried to make out the shapes of the carriages in the dim light. Many were closed, and they'd almost reached the back of the train, which stuck out from the far end of the open building like a tail in the moonlight.

"Look for an open one!" shouted Cecil. But what if Athena had sent them to the box carriages as a trap? Still, it was their only hope. Anton knew they wouldn't hear the owl behind them until it was too late, so he made himself glance back. There she was, a stealthy shadow skimming over the trains, her beak aimed like the tip of an arrow speeding toward them.

"She's coming!" yelled Anton.

"Here!" shouted Cecil. He turned sharply and leaped up to and through a narrow space in the side of one of the carriages.

Anton tried to slow and turn but found himself skidding in a slippery puddle on the pavement, his legs cycling frantically in place. He looked up and yowled as the owl locked her yellow eyes on him and dropped into a dive. Out of breath and scrambling toward the train, Anton braced for the owl's attack.

At that moment a loud hiss sounded above his head. He leaped for the opening in the carriage just as Cecil bounded out again, teeth bared and claws swiping the air, soaring over Anton's head and straight toward the owl. Athena screeched and banked awkwardly to avoid Cecil, grazing one wing against a post and tumbling in the air. The cats heard a *thud* and a fluttering shuffle in the distance.

"Come on, quick!" called Anton as Cecil landed and turned. Cecil scrambled back into the carriage, and the brothers pressed into the farthest corner of the box and waited, watching the open doorway, their hearts hammering in the silence.

Anton finally caught his breath. "Thanks," he whispered. "That was close."

"You don't have to whisper," said Cecil. "She knows we're in here."

"Maybe she's given up," Anton whispered. He couldn't help it.

Cecil sniffed and rolled his shoulders back. "She won't try again. She knows we're too tough."

"And poisonous, don't forget." Anton shivered and peered around the dusty, dark carriage. "Oh, brother. What have we gotten ourselves into?"

CHAPTER 5

A Dog's Tale

T he owl must have found some other poor creature to terrorize or lecture, and the night passed peacefully as the cat brothers settled down in the empty carriage. There wasn't anything to eat, but it was warm enough and there were a few bales of hay in one corner that made a comfortable resting place. They talked for a while, recounting the day's escapade of getting from the sailing ship to the landship, and then they drifted off to sleep. Cecil awoke when the morning sun shot a wedge of light into the narrow opening of the carriage door. It was still and silent as the light stole across the floor. First from a distance, but gradually closer, the sound of human activity drifted in. Cecil heard men talking and shouting, clanging metal, wheels turning, laughter, and something heavy being dragged this way and that.

Anton woke up and climbed off the hay bale to look out the door. "The owl was right," he said. "There are a lot of folks out there."

Cecil followed and peeked out in the opposite direction. A rolling cart piled with boxes was lumbering toward their car at a fast clip. As the cats ducked back inside, there was a shout, then an answering shout, and the cart came to a halt right in front of the sliding door to their carriage. Immediately a dog began barking in a high-pitched voice, "Back off, back off, stay away, back off this instant!"

Cecil smiled at his brother. "I bet that's one of those dogs no bigger than a shrimp."

Before Anton could reply, the door began to slide open, and two men looked inside. The cats backed up to the hay bales, making themselves as small as possible. Anton closed his eyes, since he believed humans couldn't see him when he did.

But Cecil looked on as the men began unloading boxes and canvas bags and all manner of luggage from the cart, bumping, shoving, and pulling them into the carriage.

As he was sliding one crate next to another, one of the men, who wore a cap with a bill like a duck's, looked right at Cecil and winked. "I see you," he said. Cecil didn't know what he meant, but the man appeared undisturbed, so Cecil stayed put.

When the carriage was about half-full of luggage, the duck-billed man jumped back in carrying a small crate from which the high-pitched barking of the dog continued the incessant and useless commands. "Back off. Don't do that. Back off. No. NO, NO, NO, NO!"

The man seemed amused by the racket and spoke softly when he set the crate down near the back of the carriage. Cecil observed that it had a door with a grate at the front. The slats all around the sides were a few inches apart and he could see the creature inside—a runty tan fury shouting at the top of his little lungs. "No, no, not again, no. I don't want to be in here. Back off, now. NO, NO, NO."

"You can open your eyes now," Cecil said to Anton. "They know we're here."

Anton sat up cautiously. "They do?"

"That man looked right at me," Cecil informed him.

That man was speaking softly to the dog, whose barking had faded to a low whine. The man retrieved two metal bowls, then filled one with water and poured some little tidbits that smelled like salt and dust into the other. He opened the grate carefully, and the dog, who seemed to know what was going on, backed up to the farthest reaches of the crate.

"Oh, all right. All right," he said in his high snuffly voice. "Just make sure the water bowl is full, pul-ease."

When the man had finished with the dog and closed the grate, he turned and stared openly at the two cats, who sat side by side, their tails wrapped around their legs, alert and ready to bolt.

"So how far are you going?" he asked pleasantly, but the brothers didn't understand a word. The man didn't appear alarmed in the least by their presence. He turned and went out to the cart and then came back with two more bowls and another bottle of water.

"There's not much to eat, where you're going," he said. "This'll give you a start."

And to Cecil's amazement, he filled the bowls with the tidbits and water and set them along the wall of the carriage, not far from the door. His coworker looked in and they exchanged some amused remarks, then the kind, duck-billed man climbed down and they slid the door closed. But the man didn't close it all the way. Cecil noted that he pulled it back a bit on its track, a space just big enough to let a little light and air in, and a cat, if he had a mind to leave, out.

The dog got up and lapped at his water, without speaking. Cecil sniffed, then tried a mouthful of the food in the bowl, working his jaws over it carefully. "It's not good," he pronounced. "But it's not bad."

The dog came to his grate and looked at his travel companions, his tongue out, panting. He had a dark, smushed-looking snout and big, brown, bulging eyes that made him look like he was horrified by what he saw. But evidently he wasn't.

"I've never seen cats on a train before," he said. "Did somebody put you on here? I think you must be in the wrong car."

Anton went over and looked through the bars at the little dog. "We got on by ourselves," he replied. "We're going to wherever this thing goes to help a friend in need. My name is Anton, and that's my brother Cecil."

The dog made a snuffling sound, then ran his bright pink tongue across his black lips. "What do you mean, you got on by yourselves? Animals don't just get on trains like that. And anyway, you got on the wrong car. This car is for dogs. Obviously."

"That man seemed to think it was for cats, too," Cecil observed from his station by the food bowl. "He brought us dinner."

The dog snorted. "He's just uninformed. Cats and dogs don't travel together. Everybody knows that."

"Have you been on a train before?" Anton asked.

"I've made this trip five times, and I don't like it one bit."

"It doesn't seem so bad to me," said Cecil. "There's lots of room and they serve meals. It takes you where you want to go. I like it fine."

"That's easy for you to say," the dog replied. "You're not stuck in a steaming hot box."

"Yeah," Anton agreed. "That's not so great."

A loud whistle interrupted this conversation, followed by a ringing bell. A powerful vibration ran across the floor, followed by a rough, clanking jolt to the whole car, first one way, then the other. A man shouted something.

"We're pulling out of the station," the dog informed Anton. "There's no turning back now."

Cecil dashed to the door and looked out as the chuffing sound grew louder and a hot blast of air swept in from outside. "Whoa," he said. "So this is a landship . . . I mean, a train. It's amazing!"

Anton was studying the latch on the dog's crate. "What's your name?" he said, as he brought his paw to the metal plate.

"I'm Willy," said the dog.

"Well, Willy," Anton said. "I think you may be glad you got to travel with a couple of cats."

Willy, panting miserably, didn't seem to notice Anton's paw working around the latch. "I guess it will kill time to have somebody to talk to," he admitted.

"You can give us the benefit of your travel experience," Anton agreed.

Cecil, turning away from the view, joined his brother at the crate and peered in. He saw that there was a blanket folded at the back, and something round and red in one corner. He thought it must be some stuff to keep the dog comfortable while he traveled.

Cecil watched Anton's paw on the latch and recalled the time he'd opened a pirate's chest by pressing on the lid. "Try pushing on it," he suggested.

Anton slid his paw along the latch, pressing and pressing. "I'm not getting anywhere," he said.

Willy finally noticed Anton's paw. "Hey, what are you doing to my cage?" he snapped. "You don't know anything about these; they're for dogs. You'll break it, and then I'll never get out!"

"Let me give it a try," said Cecil, ignoring Willy. Anton stepped back and Cecil studied the latch for a moment before placing his paw on one end. The latch was just a metal bar that dropped into an open slot. "If we let you out, will you be polite?" he asked Willy.

"Let me out?" cried Willy, looking from Cecil to Anton and back. "Can you really do that? I'd be crazy with gratitude!" He did a couple of quick spins in the crate.

Cecil slid his paw down to the far end of the bar and pressed. It lifted with a clink and the door swung open. "There you go," he said.

Willy was awestruck. For a moment all he could do was drop his mouth open and roll his bulgy eyes. But as Cecil pushed the door away, he hurtled out of the cage into the wide-open space of the carriage.

"You did it," he barked. "You did it. I'm free." He ran with abandon, up one side of the car and down the other. "I love cats!" he shouted. "Cats are great!"

Anton and Cecil watched him, smiling smugly at each other. The chuffing noise had settled into a deep snore and they could see the scenery passing by, speeding up now as the train left the bustling city behind. Willy continued racing up and down.

"Dogs are weird," Cecil said.

Willy made a few more wild circuits and then slowed to a trot. He went to the water bowl the man had left for the cats and lapped up half of it.

"This is the way to travel," he said, approaching Anton and Cecil. He stretched his front legs down and raised his back legs, snuffling gleefully. He had a silly, curly tail that quivered in the air. Then he sat down with a grunt and addressed the brothers. "I am now prepared to entertain any questions you cats may have about train travel. I can also enlighten you about the many interesting characters and places you may encounter on your journey."

"I thought you didn't want to go," said Cecil.

Willy chuckled. "I just hate that box and I always protest injustice in the strongest possible terms. I actually look forward to my destination, which is the family home of my young mistress, who is traveling in one of the other carriages." He lifted one back foot and scratched at his ear. "In the winter we live in the city, which has its charms, but in the summer I spend my time in the open and come and go as I please."

"What is the open like?" Anton asked.

"Very open," Willy replied.

Cecil groaned. "I'm unenlightened," he said.

"Are there no buildings?" Anton asked. "Are there no trees?"

"Near the house there are trees and a road. But beyond that it's all tall grass, taller than any of us, waving and rustling like water, as far as you can see in any direction. An ocean of swaying golden grass. That's the open. One can scare up all sorts of little frightened creatures that live in holes."

"Mice?" Cecil said.

"Some are mouse-like. Some are furry and chatter a lot. There are turtles, which can bite. I avoid those. Little snakes. I've caught a few of those. And there are all manner of large creatures as well."

"Like horses?"

"Horses are generally kept inside fences. But in the open there are animals with hooves, smaller than horses, some with horns growing out of their heads. They run away when approached. There are also animals that resemble dogs but are not exactly dogs. I've never met one, nor do I hope to, as they are large and travel in groups making a great deal of noise, especially at night, when they howl in a most unseemly way."

"How do you know they're not dogs?" Cecil asked. In his view there was too much variety among animals called dogs, some big, some tiny, and all manner of noses and tails. But presumably dogs knew dogs when they saw them.

"Well, for one thing they live in the open, and run wild all the time. No human wants them around. In fact they chase them away. I always hide when I see one. It must be a very different sort of life they lead. They eat whatever they can catch!"

Cecil smiled. "They're hunters. I think I like these dogs."

Willy snuffed and bugged out his eyes. "They're *not* dogs, that's the point. Humans call them coyotes."

"Coyotes!" Anton and Cecil exclaimed.

"Have you met any?"

"No," Anton said. "But we're looking for one. We're trying to find a friend and he lives between a coyote and a whale."

"Well, there are a lot of coyotes," said Willy. "I don't know how you'll find the right one."

"No," Anton agreed, looking at Cecil, who grunted and shook his head. The whistle shrieked and the train seemed to shudder as it slowed down to travel around a bend.

Willy walked over to the door and stuck his head out. "We're coming into a little town."

"Do you get off here?" asked Cecil.

"Oh no," said Willy. "I'll be with you all day and all night. We'll get to my stop tomorrow morning. I'm not sure where the train goes after that, but I know it's not the end of the line."

"The end of the line," Anton repeated.

"I once traveled with a very superior dog who was going all the way. He told me there was a city and a lot of water at the end. Which is why it's the end. After that you have to take a ship. I don't think I'd like that."

"No, you wouldn't," said Anton.

"Yes, you would," said Cecil.

"Don't tell me you cats have been on a ship?" Willy exclaimed.

"We have," Anton said.

"Well, we've got all day and all night," Willy said. He trotted to the back of the carriage and curled up on some of the hay. "I love a good story. Tell me all about it."

And so they did, while the small towns and forests and fields drifted by. Willy listened, snuffling now and then, or asking a question, and the brothers described their separate adventures and eventual reunion. "That is one great story," Willy said, as shadows crept across the floor and the sun began to set. They agreed to finish their meals and then dog and cats settled down for a long sleep. In the morning, after much whistling and shouting and screeching of brakes, the train pulled into a building with a long platform and a great many passengers began to disembark. Willy made a dash for the crate and got inside.

Soon the man with the duck-bill cap appeared and leaped up into the carriage, intent on Willy's crate. When he saw the door standing open he gave a soft humph of surprise.

"How did this get opened?" he said. He turned,

resting his hands on his hips, and addressed Anton and Cecil. "I don't suppose you two know anything about this." Cecil was very busy washing his face and Anton pretended great interest in the wooden ceiling of the carriage. The man looked back at Willy, who was sitting quietly before his empty bowls, his tongue hanging out, panting woefully. "Well, no harm done," the man said, closing the grate and dropping the latch. "Your lady is waiting."

When he bent to pick up the crate, Willy rushed to the front, barking in the high-pitched voice Anton and Cecil now knew to be the height of theatrics. "NO, NO, NO," he barked. "Get back. Get away from this box. NO, NO. This is an outrage."

As man and dog disappeared out the door, Cecil stopped pawing over his face and turned to Anton. "Dogs are so weird," he said.

❖ ❖ ❖

The train clattered over the wide, serene plains with a great arc of steam trailing behind. As it rumbled solemnly along its route, Anton noticed that creatures of all sizes turned to take a look. The animals seemed wary of it. Thin, springy deer and colorful chickens scattered ahead of the train as it barreled across the land. Humans often stopped their work and watched its progress from one horizon to the other, sometimes raising a hand in greeting. Anton wondered if they made an odd picture: two cats, one black and one gray, sitting side by side in a boxcar doorway, gazing out at the world as the train rolled steadfastly by.

It was cooler in the breeze at the doorway, though not much. Between naps, Anton sat with his tail curled around his front paws and pondered the brown and green fields, mile after mile. It had only been three days of traveling, and though the carriage could be sweltering at times, the duck-billed hat man brought them water and food whenever the train stopped, so at least they weren't starving. Even so, Anton felt uneasy. He was beginning to doubt the reliability of the mouse network.

"You know what we will never see out here?"

Cecil shook his head. "A nice crab dinner?"

"A whale," said Anton. "There will never be a whale out here, because as far as I can see," he gestured with a paw, "there is no ocean."

"That's okay. You can't really eat a whale, anyway."

Anton sighed. "But we need one if we're going to figure out 'between the whale and the coyote' to find Hieronymus."

"Oh. Right. Don't worry about that, we'll find him." Cecil stuck his head all the way out so his fur rippled in the breeze.

"You're going to fall," Anton warned, carefully leaning away from the open door. "You'll hit your head on something out there."

"It feels good!" called Cecil, his voice warbling in the draft. He turned to face forward, his eyes squeezed almost shut. "Hey, I see something."

"What is it? Wait, let me guess. You see an end-less field of waving grass."

"No. Well, yes, there's that. But also there's—" Cecil's voice was carried off by the wind.

"What?" yelled Anton.

Cecil pulled his head back inside the carriage. "There's a town up ahead, looks like a fairly big one. I bet we stop there."

The brothers stepped over to the heap of straw in the far corner and burrowed behind it. A stop usually meant men coming on board to load and unload cargo. Sometimes the men were friendly and sometimes they were not, so it was better to hide. The train slowed and finally pulled to a halt with a last great sigh of steam. From outside the carriage came the sounds of a lively town—shouts, barks, bells, rolling cart wheels, even a thread of music, perhaps from a nearby saloon. Mixed in with the scents of metal and smoke from the train were the strong smells of horses, dirt-packed roads, and food cooking.

Cecil squirmed in the straw. "I hope the man brings us one of those things with the meats and cheeses smashed inside the bread," he murmured. "I like those."

"Shh," whispered Anton. "Someone's coming."

The duck-billed man climbed through the doorway and spoke.

"Fellas?" he called softly. "This is as far as we go."

Anton and Cecil poked their heads out of the straw and looked at the man expectantly. He gestured with his thumb, holding it sideways in the air and waving it.

"What's he saying?" asked Cecil.

"Don't know," said Anton. "Something about his paw."

The man took a few steps toward them, and the cats saw with disappointment that he'd brought them no food this time.

"Come on, now," said the man gently. "End of

the line." He raised and lowered both arms in a sweeping motion toward the open door. The cats' eyes followed the flapping arms.

"Maybe he's telling us about something outside," Cecil suggested.

"Like a bird?"

"Like one of those owls."

"He's warning us!" said Anton. "Oh, that's very good of him." They both nestled back down into the straw.

There was a shout from outside and the man shrugged. "All right then. Suit yourself." He turned and jumped down from the carriage. A few minutes of quiet were followed by a jolting clunk that shook the cats to their bones. They heard a high-pitched whistle and a loud hiss of steam, which usually meant they were on their way again, but this time the carriage didn't move. They heard the chuffing pulse start up, deep and booming at first but then beginning to fade.

"What's going on?" said Anton. "That doesn't sound right."

Cecil leaped from the straw and shook out his fur. "Let's take a look." He trotted to the doorway and peered around the edge, his white-tipped tail flicking from side to side. "Oh, cat's whiskers!" he gasped.

"What is it?" asked Anton, clambering out of the straw. "Is it an owl?"

Cecil crouched and stuck his head farther out. "No, it's the engine. It left us behind!"

"Left us?" cried Anton, pushing in beside Cecil to see if this news could possibly be true.

"Can you believe that?" said Cecil. "It just . . . unhooked from the rest and moved onto another path, straight through that gate there." He sat back and looked at Anton uncertainly. "So what's going to pull us now?"

Anton shook his head slowly. The ways of trains were still a mystery. He peeked out again and saw that nightfall was coming, the sun hovering low on the horizon, directly over the rails that ran as far as he could see in the distance. *At least we're still headed in the right direction,* he thought, *toward Hieronymus, into the land of the setting sun. Though we've got to* move *to get there.*

A mechanical whine arose inside the gate where the engine had gone, and the brothers craned their necks to see what was happening. Loud squeaks from rubbing metal plates and rusted wheels rang out as the section of rail beneath the engine moved by itself in a smooth circle. Then the familiar rumble of the engine began again, and Cecil and Anton saw its pointed prow emerge from the gate, now facing out.

"They turned it around!" marveled Cecil. "How did they do that? Actually, *why* did they do that?"

Anton only shook his head again. He felt as if the noise would break his ears into pieces before this was over. The engine chugged through the gate but traveled on a track alongside the other carriages, moving slowly and, from Anton's point of view, the wrong way.

"Now what?" he asked, shrinking back as the engine lumbered past their hiding place, so close they could have jumped onto it.

"No idea," said Cecil, leaning out of the doorway to watch the man in the window of the engine. "That must be the Captain, there."

The engine puffed past the end of the line of carriages and switched over to the set of rails it had rolled in on. It slowly backed up toward the standing train until the two smashed together with a jarring crunch. A man on the ground reached up and adjusted the metal connectors behind the engine, then stood back and yelled to the Captain, waving a flag on a small stick over his head. The Captain appeared at the window and nodded, pulling a cord attached to a bell to make it ring and ring.

Cecil swayed at the doorway to keep his balance, then turned to Anton, his golden eyes glinting in the sunset. "Hey, you want to know what I think?"

"I'm going to regret saying yes, aren't I?" said Anton.

"I think it's time to get off this particular landship."

Anton was startled. "Get off? Why?"

Cecil looked down the side of the train again. "No time to explain." The shrill whistle blew and Cecil bounded out of the carriage, landing in the dirt next to the rails. "Come on," he called to Anton.

Anton looked at him in a panic. "Cecil! Get back up here! What are you doing?"

"I'm trying to keep our mission going. Come with me!"

"No! We have to stay on. It's the only way we

have to travel!" The great chuffing sounds began and the train started to move.

Anton's stomach did a somersault.

The train was moving in the wrong direction.

"But, how . . ." Anton began.

"Don't worry about how," Cecil said quickly, trotting on the ground below. "Just get off the train."

The man with the flag spotted Cecil on the ground and stepped toward him, swatting at him with the flag to drive him away from the grinding wheels. Cecil ducked around the man and began to lope next to the train, calling up to Anton. "You have to jump out! Come on, you can do it!"

Anton was paralyzed. He realized that Cecil was right, that the train was going back to where it had come from. If he stayed on it he'd never find Hieronymus, and maybe he would lose Cecil as well. But the train was picking up speed, and looking down was making him dizzy. The ground seemed very far away.

"Anton!" yelled Cecil, falling behind the pace of the train. "Jump now!"

Anton gathered all four paws together at the very edge of the doorway and leaned out. The huge, undulating wheels were so close—if he fell into one of them he'd be ground to bits. The carriage bumped and swayed on the rails. Dust flew up into his nose and eyes. He hunched his shoulders and looked back at Cecil desperately, but Cecil couldn't help him. Every passing second stretched the distance between them, and still he hesitated. Hieronymus's pointed little face rose up in his mind. *What kind of rescuer am I if I can't even rescue myself?*

He tensed every muscle in his body, gathered his courage, squeezed his eyes shut, and with a yowl from deep in his chest, he hurled himself from the train.

CHAPTER 6

Cat Overboard

Sometime during the night it began to rain in drenching bucketfuls, washing streams of mud across the rails, pounding on the roofs of the train carriages, puddling in the dirt tracks where horses and humans traversed. Anton and Cecil had taken refuge in a large space underneath a house near the train yard, but low, rolling thunder boomed over the plains and shook the two cats awake from their fitful napping again and again. A stack of pallets kept them off the wet ground, and the brothers wrapped themselves into tight balls next to each other, trying to sleep, waiting out the storm.

At first light, Cecil opened one eye at the sound of two men stomping up the wooden steps and into the house above his head. Soon he saw the feet of more people traipsing up while others came down, and there was a steady tromping back and forth inside the house. The rain still fell at a drizzle but nothing like the night before. Anton stirred and sat up, gazing around groggily. He began cleaning his filthy fur, starting with his ears.

Cecil regarded his brother and suppressed a chuckle. "Old Billy has a saying, you know. He says, 'Cats always land paws down.'" He smiled. "You sure proved that one wrong, didn't you?"

Anton glared at Cecil and continued with his bath. "Let's see what part *you* land on next time *you* jump out of a moving train. I'm lucky to be alive."

Cecil flicked his tail with the memory. "I didn't think you'd ever stop rolling. And that *screech* when you jumped! It was as loud as our old buddy Athena. Impressive." He attempted a grave expression. "Seriously, how do you feel?"

Anton arched his back and stretched his hind legs one at a time. "Battered, but I'll be fine. Hungry, though." He looked toward the steps. "What's all the commotion?"

"I was wondering the same thing. It seems to be a popular place."

They jumped off the pallets and peered up through the slatted steps. The people coming out of the door were laden with baskets and packages, and the cats caught the distinct scents of cheese and bread. A few men stood talking on the porch above, gesturing with their hands and eating something that smelled delicious.

Cecil trotted back and forth with his neck craned, his tail curling in anticipation. "If we're lucky . . ."

Plop. A chunk of meat and cheese fell through the slats in the steps to the ground in front of them.

"Excellent." Cecil beamed, bounding over to the snack.

"Great cats." Anton looked up again as a crust of bread glanced off his shoulder. "Humans are so messy."

✤ ✤ ✤

The cats waited until the crowd had thinned before slipping away from the house and back to the train yard. They ducked under the platform to avoid the ruckus above as well as the relentless drizzle, and watched for activity on the rails. Hours passed and only a single train came rumbling in, this one with just a few carriages. Cecil watched as the engine somehow got itself turned around and connected to the back end, chugging off the way it had come, just like the train they'd traveled on.

"Do they never keep going?" Anton complained, gazing in the opposite direction. "There are rails going that way. Why don't the trains continue on?"

Cecil shifted in the damp air, his eyes half-closed. "I don't know. What if we've reached the end?"

"The end of what?" asked Anton stubbornly.

"The end of this journey," said Cecil. "Maybe Hieronymus is here in this town, or maybe we've already passed him." He turned to Anton. "Have you thought of that?"

Anton's mouth opened and closed again. "No, we're not at the end, for goodness' sake. We haven't seen a whale, haven't met a coyote, haven't found any sign of Hieronymus, obviously." He looked away, shaking his head.

Cecil's ear cocked sideways and his body tensed at the sound of a mouse-like scurrying off to his left. He turned his head swiftly and caught a glimpse of three fluffs of brown-gray fur, one bigger than the other two, hurrying along the far side of the platform. Cecil's mouth watered, but he shook his head. *You're on a mouse-free diet for now, remember?* he told himself. Still, mice could be useful.

"Hey!" he shouted at the mice. They jumped and scurried faster.

Anton looked over Cecil's head. "You're scaring them." He raised his voice a little. "Excuse me!" he called. The bigger mouse quickly pushed the two little ones ahead of it through a crack in the beam. Anton persisted. "Are you in the mouse network?"

The mouse's tail vanished into the crack. Several seconds passed in silence, then a high, quavering voice spoke from the direction of the beam.

"And what in the world do you think you know about the mouse network?" said the voice.

Anton stood but moved no closer. "We received a message at our home very far away," he said. "Via mouse. Mice, actually."

A tiny nose protruded from the crack, followed

by two black, shining eyes. "Cats? You're trying to tell me a pair of *cats* got a network message?"

"Yes." Anton nodded. "And now we're trying to travel west into the land of the setting sun, but the trains all seem to stop here, and we can't find our friend. Can you help us?"

The pink nose swung from side to side, and the voice squeaked louder. "I don't know who you are, but you're not fooling me one bit. Mice working with cats? Please. You all are nothing but a menace to me and my family, and the sooner you're gone, or dead, the better off we'll all be."

At that, Cecil sat up. "Rude," he said to Anton, "but it's a fair point."

Anton ignored his brother. "But, sir . . ."

"It's ma'am," said the mouse.

". . . of course," stammered Anton. "Ma'am, if you'd just tell us about the trains we'd be out of your way."

But there came only silence from the beam.

Cecil gave an elaborate sigh. "This is what I'm talking about, Anton. Is Hieronymus the only polite mouse left in the world?"

A scuffle came from the crack. "Hieronymus?" cried the mouse. "Now hold on a second, you know Hieronymus?"

"We do," said Anton. "He's our friend, and he called for us to come and help him."

"Well, why didn't you say so?" she asked.

"Would it have made a difference?" asked Cecil dryly.

"Of course it would have," replied the mouse, edging a bit farther out of the beam. "He saved the lives of two of my children in a real gutsy standoff with a hawk. It was a sight to see. He just *talked* that hawk into sparing those pups, sure as shootin'." She paused, passing her tail across her eyes and sniffing. "I'll never be able to repay him."

"Well, how about you repay *us*, with information," suggested Cecil, "and then we'll repay *him* for you by rescuing him."

The mouse nodded and raised her sliver of a paw to point down the empty track. "You're on the right path. He went that way last time I saw him. Said he was going to find a second cousin, I believe."

"Yes," said Anton, "but no trains go that way. How did he *go*?"

"We call 'em 'cloud riders,'" the mouse said. "They come in from that direction and leave again. That's how he went."

"Great!" exclaimed Cecil. "When?"

"Maybe today, maybe tomorrow, you never can say. Have patience." The mouse retreated, then poked her head out once more. "A little advice, though. Stay out of sight. The humans don't care for the likes of any of us on the cloud riders. They even put dogs in cages."

Anton nodded. "Got it."

"Best of luck to you. And be careful. I hear tales from the mice who come from that land, stories of dark and fearsome creatures who live in the mountains." The mouse's whiskers twitched. "Creatures big enough to eat a cat, so they say."

"Hmmm," said Cecil, rubbing one ear with a paw. "Do they *want* to eat a cat?"

But the mouse had disappeared. The two cats curled their front paws underneath their chests and arranged their tails alongside their bodies for warmth. As the sun began to set, Cecil gave a tremendous yawn. He forced himself to stay awake a little longer so he and Anton could watch the rails, waiting for a train to ride in on a cloud.

❖ ❖ ❖

As the afternoon wore on, Anton napped despite his intention to remain alert. He dreamed that he was curled comfortably on his old quilt in the lighthouse back home, when his mother Sonya rushed in, her eyes wide and frightened. She told him there was a creature outside on the path, a great beast the color of smoke with red eyes and rows of sharp teeth. *This is the one that eats cats,* Anton informed his mother in the dream, a terror creeping over him. He and Sonya listened to the creature breathing—a deep, rolling rumble moving steadily closer. They trembled in a corner as the beast screamed, high and shrill, until Anton thought his ears would split. He felt Sonya nudge him repeatedly, until finally he woke up and realized that it was Cecil prodding him, and the scream was the whistle of a long train pulling in to the yard, arriving imperiously in a cloud of steam.

"This is it," called Cecil over the noise. And he was right—the train had come from the direction of the setting sun.

"But wait," said Anton, getting to his feet stiffly. "We have to see if it turns around."

"Hmmm," said Cecil, frowning. "If you say so."

As they watched, a crowd of humans gathered near the tracks. Most of the carriages on this train were different from those they'd noticed before. These were long with many square windows lining the sides, and the tops resembled the roofs of houses, peaked instead of flat. People waved hands and handkerchiefs out of the windows to others on the ground as the train hissed to a stop.

"Let's get out from under here so we can see better," said Anton.

Cecil led the way and the two cats dashed from the safety of the platform to the side wall of the gated roundhouse. The drizzle had turned back to driving rain so they crouched under the eaves as best they could and gazed at the chaotic scene. The platform was packed with humans, most wearing hats and standing next to large trunks. They held bags, baskets, and children in their arms and watched the men in the yard opening the doors. Other people stepped out of the train and pushed their way through the crowd. Sure enough, a heavy clanking issued from behind the engine, and slowly, slowly, it separated from the rest, chugged over to a side track, and began to back up toward the roundhouse gate.

"Yep, it'll turn around in there and then pull on out," said Cecil confidently. "This is our ride, sure as shootin'."

"How will we ever get on?" said Anton. Humans

swarmed everywhere, and there were only a few of the familiar box-like carriages attached down at the far end. Yard workers busily hauled boxes and crates in and out of the open doors.

"Things will calm down a bit," replied Cecil. "I hope."

But the frenetic activity continued, and the workers closed the doors to the box carriages tightly and latched them. The engine emerged from the round-house, rear end first, backing toward the waiting chain. The two met and connected with a clang.

"Time's up," said Anton. "We've got to do something."

"Quick," said Cecil. "We'll jump into one of those." He lifted his head toward the windowed carriages.

"But the humans!" called Anton as they began to run. "Remember what the mouse said?"

"No choice!" yelled Cecil. "Watch out for the Captain!"

Anton knew Cecil meant the man with the flat hat who was striding along inspecting the wheels and greeting passengers. The two cats ducked next to a stack of crates as he passed, then leaped up the stairs and into the carriage.

"Hide!" Cecil called over his shoulder. "Anywhere, just like we did on the ship."

Anton glimpsed a long room with windows on both walls and bright lights hanging from the ceilings. It was full of people sitting in large chairs and talking loudly to one another, their hats bobbing as they nodded and turned to hold their hands up to the windows. Quick as a wink he slipped into a forest of bags and folds of clothing that hung to the floor under the seats where the humans sat. The hanging cloth was of many different varieties— some soft as his sleeping quilt, some cold and shimmery or rough and stiff, and some made from the fur of animals. Carefully avoiding the many legs and feet along the floor, he pressed himself into a ball, motionless against one wall of the carriage, shifting only when a sharp heel or toe came too near.

❧ ❧ ❧

Cecil, for his part, did much the same on the other side of the carriage, though his bulk was harder to conceal than his brother's. Something overpoweringly sweet in the air tickled his nose and he almost sneezed, but he shook his head vigorously until the feeling went away. Peering out from under a swath of white fabric with short lengths of string swinging at the edge, he searched for Anton along the floor but didn't see him. *He couldn't have gone far,* Cecil told himself. They'd just sit tight and stay in hiding, then they'd figure out what to do next.

Soon enough the doors to the carriage clanged shut, the bell rang, and the train began to move, chugging slowly and then faster in its rhythmic pattern. After the last light of day faded from the windows, the humans were brought plates of fruit, bread, and chicken-like meat. To Cecil's disappointment, none dropped into his hiding place.

The night passed on and the carriage grew quiet. Cecil guessed the humans were sleeping, but he didn't want to risk emerging to look for Anton. Stuffed against the wall and surrounded by clothing and shoes, Cecil squirmed uncomfortably. His coarse black fur was still damp from the rain, and he was hungry, as always. He finally rested his chin on his paws and dozed for a time, awakening to a brightening in the windows and general shuffling among the passengers.

A sharp voice cut through the quiet of the carriage and Cecil ventured a peek out. It was the Captain, wearing his flat hat and striding slowly along, speaking to the people on either side as he went. Cecil pulled in quickly and buried his face in his paws. *If I stay still, there's no way he'll notice me down here.* The Captain moved closer and continued his chatter, and Cecil wondered if Anton was as well hidden as he was. They were making good progress—it would be a shame for Anton to give them away now.

The Captain stepped right next to Cecil's hiding place and spoke to the man and lady in the chairs above him. The lady rose slightly from her seat, perhaps to grasp hands with the Captain as humans often did with one another, and as she sat back down she swept the folds of her dress together. Cecil felt an odd chill on his posterior, and realized that his tail was suddenly exposed to the open air. Quickly he tucked it underneath him, but it was too late. The lady let out a piercing shriek and leaped to her feet.

"Good heavens, what is it, madam?" cried the Captain, leaning over to look.

"A skunk!" wailed the lady. "There's a skunk under my seat!"

As the lady stumbled away, Cecil was revealed and he felt all eyes upon him. More people screamed and Cecil scrambled to hide again, but there was nowhere to go. He dashed this way and that, but it was a tight space and the humans were swiping at him with bags and walking sticks as if he were some kind of horror. Hadn't they ever seen a cat before?

Cecil dove for an opening between two pairs of legs but he was blocked by a shiny boot. A large hand grasped the fur behind his head and hauled him up in the air, and another hand clamped around his chest.

"I've got it!" yelled the Captain. "Calm down, everyone, I'll take care of this. Just keep calm." He held Cecil as far away from his face as he could and strode swiftly to the door of the carriage. Cecil knew he had no time left.

"Anton!" Cecil yowled, struggling in the Captain's grasp. "Don't come out! Stay hidden and I'll find you at the next stop!" He hoped like crazy that Anton could hear him.

The Captain reached the door and yanked it open with one hand, then stepped into the space between carriages and turned. Cecil could see the land rolling swiftly by as the wind whipped past them and the wheels clacked deafeningly over the tracks.

"Off you go, Mr. Stowaway, back where you be-long," said the Captain.

He grasped Cecil with both hands and tossed him, firmly and without hesitation, in an arc through the air and over the tall prairie grass.

CHAPTER 7

Prairie Town

I'*ve just been thrown off a train,* Cecil thought as he flew. *This is turning out to be quite an adventure.*

He swiveled his body midflight and landed softly in the waving grass, right on his paws.

The grass was tall. That was the chief problem with it—it was taller than Cecil. Otherwise, it was soft and easy enough to move through, and sweet-smelling in a way. But after plowing ahead for a bit and finding no end or edge to it, Cecil stopped. Stuck in the middle of a field of the stuff, he was bound to get lost or go round in circles.

The dust in the grass tickled his nose and he sneezed, which didn't help matters. A small flock of birds fluttered by overhead, sparking an idea. *I've got to get a better view,* he thought, and he tensed his springy back legs and jumped straight up above the wispy tops of the grasses, glancing around quickly as he did so. A wide vista of emptiness, with a few hills and low trees on the horizon. *Hmmm. Where's the train?* Cecil faced the opposite direction and jumped again.

Ah! There were the train tracks, on a rise at the edge of the field. That was good. He sprang up again and looked down the rails to his left. Nothing. Once more up, turning right. Far in the distance he spotted the plume of smoke from the train, drifting to join the clouds overhead, the engine disappearing behind the hills. *Anton's still on that train,* Cecil thought. *That's my path.* He'd noticed that the rails were set on raised ground where no grass grew, so he pushed through the green stalks, leaping every so often to check his bearings, until he stood upon one of the massive wooden beams set in the ground under the tracks. From there he gazed about.

After days of nonstop train rumbling, dog yapping,

and human chatter, the quiet was profound. Wide swaths of grass stretched away from the rails in all directions, flecked with small flowers in bunches of blues, reds, and yellows, spreading across hillsides and filling ditches. Pushed into swells by the wind, the grasses swayed in a way that made Cecil think of the sea, and with a pang in his belly he realized how much he missed seeing and being out on the water. The *sshushh* of the breeze in the fields and the faint buzzing of insects were all he could hear, and he felt strange, unsettled. He'd never been completely alone like this, without food or companions, even human ones, in the middle of nowhere. Would anyone know if something were to happen to him? Would Anton?

Cecil gave himself a thorough shake, ears to tail. *Come on,* he told himself. *Time to explore.* He set off along the rail bed, trotting in the dirt to spare his paws, following the path of Anton's train. *Somebody who knows this place will come along here pretty soon,* he assured himself. *Something will turn up.* But as the wind plucked at his ears and slipped through his fur, he shivered despite the warmth of the day. He could see a very long way ahead as the rails snaked through the undulating grass, and he wasn't at all sure that anything would turn up.

⅌ ⅌ ⅌

The sun had warmed Cecil's tail and backside all morning and it now beamed down on his face energetically as it traveled the same route as the rails. He had started out at a trot, but by early afternoon he plodded along the treeless track in the unsparing heat. His ears drooped, his tongue thickened; even his nose felt dry. He kept an eye out for water or anything that looked edible, but so far had seen only birds and a few fast-moving rabbits from a distance. The waving grasses thinned to bare tracts in some places, clearings of sandy dirt strewn with small and large piles of rocks. A couple of darting lizards chased each other through the crevices, but Cecil didn't have the energy to pursue them. No easy supply of fish or crabs out here, that was for sure.

Good grief, I am *getting soft, just like Anton always says.* Cecil squinted ahead once again to see if he could spy a town or train stop coming up, but the rails wound away into more of the same green-brown landscape. A faint sparkle caught the sunlight off to his right—something he thought might be a pond or pool. He struck off through the grasses and emerged in a meadow of stubbly plants and rounded mounds of earth dotted with holes. Just past the mounds was a clump of small bushes next to a pond of rippling water, beckoning to his parched tongue. Cecil hesitated. A sense that he was being watched quivered his whiskers, though he didn't see anyone. The holes in the ground were fairly large, big enough for a cat certainly, but not for anything much bigger. He chose a path between them and started toward the pond, treading quietly, staying low.

A scrabble and a flash of something off to his left made him jump, but when he turned his head it was gone. He padded faster. Another movement behind him, and this time he caught the barest glimpse of a little head, yellow and furry, before it popped back down into a hole. Cecil jogged the rest of the way to the pond and circled around to the far side, gratefully lapping up the cool water while keeping his eyes fixed on the mounds. Moments passed with no movement from the holes.

Then suddenly a voice piped up from directly behind him. "Hello?"

Cecil sprang sideways, his tail fur puffed and water dripping from his face. "Gah!" he spluttered. Next to the pond was a creature about half his size sitting up on its hind legs, with golden-brown fur, wide, dark brown eyes, tiny flat ears on the sides of its round head, and a stumpy black tail. Its paws were tipped with long black claws that looked useful for digging. The creature placed one front paw on the ground, as if poised to spring away.

"Sorry to startle you," it said in a clipped, high-pitched voice. "But we're curious to know what you are." Its inquisitive eyes took in Cecil's pointed ears, white whiskers, paintbrush tail.

Cecil shook the water from his face and raised his head. "I'm a cat."

"A cat?" The creature cocked its head as if measuring this news against what he was seeing.

Cecil swung his tail. "Friendly." He gestured toward the pond. "Just thirsty."

The furry creature nodded, lifted his face to the sky, and gave out several short yips in a repeated pattern. Cecil heard a scraping and shuffling in the mounds, and other heads delivering answering yips popped up from the holes. A few here, more over there, until there were dozens, large and small, scampering over to line the edge of the pond, all chattering and watching Cecil with interest. Their voices overlapped one another in quick, excited exchanges. *It says it's a cat! Look at its ears! Look at its tail! A baby cat? What about the long black fur? Is it lost? So little!*

Cecil took issue with the comments. "I'm not a *baby*," he said to the first creature. "I'm actually huge, for a cat."

At this the whole clan tittered. *He says he's HUGE! Did you hear that? A huge cat.*

"You are small compared to some cats we know," said the creature, smiling.

"Well, what are *you*?" asked Cecil. He felt a little nervous confronted by so many of whatever they were.

"We are prairie dogs. I'm Jojo."

"I'm Cecil. You're dogs?" Cecil gazed around at them, sitting tall on their stubby hind legs. "You don't look like the dogs I know." A group of young pups in the front row giggled so hard they fell over onto their tails.

"Where have you come from?" asked Jojo, eyeing him closely.

Cecil pointed with his paw, and then paused.

How to tell them? "I'm from a land far away, across the ocean."

The prairie dogs exploded with chatter. *Did he say ocean? What's an ocean? Is it a village? How far away?*

Cecil gestured widely. "The ocean is . . . really big water, like if this pond covered all of this land." The prairie dogs gasped and shrank back. "I traveled by ship, and then by train to get here." He pointed to the raised rails in the distance as the crowd wailed and shook their heads.

Jojo pulled his head back in surprise. "You traveled on the thundercloud? You did this alone?"

Cecil shook his head. A jolt of worry surged through him—had Anton made it to the next station? Was he waiting there? "I was with my brother," he explained. "But we got separated." The prairie dogs immediately sat up with stricken faces, peering in all directions as if they might be able to spy the brother cat. Jojo turned and yipped to several of the others, who dashed away to the holes. They returned with their paws full and placed before Cecil an array of grasses, seeds, flower buds, and dead insects. Cecil looked at Jojo for guidance.

"You must be hungry," said Jojo. "Have some of our food."

"Oh," said Cecil, looking at the pile doubtfully. "Thank you." Flowers as food? He used his claws to fish out a few grasshoppers and beetles—he could eat those at least. After a time, the bigger prairie dogs skittered off to other tasks, keeping an eye on the black cat in their midst, but the younger pups stayed around the pond, creeping as close to Cecil as they dared. Cecil noticed that the series of holes went on as far as he could see—*there must be a whole town of these creatures,* he thought.

"Will you play a game with us?" the pups asked, hopping joyfully.

"What kind of game?" asked Cecil.

"Just watch," said one.

"Look at what we can do," said another. They scampered to the nearest mounds and disappeared into the holes. Cecil stood before the mounds and waited. *Do they want me to follow them down there?* he wondered. *Is it hide-and-seek?* Suddenly a pup popped up, giggling raucously. Cecil stepped toward her and in a flash she disappeared again. Another popped up from a different hole, chittering at Cecil. *Oh I see!* He grinned. *A game of catch.*

Cecil sprang toward the second pup but he, too, was gone in an instant. More pups appeared, first in front of him and then behind, teasing with their little squeaks and yips and then ducking back out of sight. At first Cecil was a step too slow each time, but he quickly learned to anticipate their moves. He crouched low next to a hole and waited, his tail swishing, and when the pup peeked out he swiftly tapped it on the head with his paw. "Got you!" he laughed. The pups shrieked, trying to outwit Cecil, but he only got better, once tagging three of them in rapid succession. Finally he collapsed next to the mounds in exhaustion, chuckling all over again when the pups rushed over and sat on his belly, begging him for a story. After a drink from the pond, he curled his tail over his front paws and recounted a lively tale about a pirate ship, a stolen jewel, and a daring rope swing across the dark sea.

Jojo lingered nearby, listening attentively until the story was finished. "May I ask, what do you usually eat, if not flowers?"

"I eat a lot of fish," Cecil admitted, "when I can get them." He recalled the mouse's warning about things that ate cats. "So, does anything eat *you*, out here?" he asked.

The prairie pups yipped and growled in a show of bravery, but Jojo's dark eyes grew serious. "Lots of things," he said. "Eagles and falcons, badgers and ferrets, rattlesnakes." He paused. "Lynxes."

"Lynxes?" said Cecil. "What are they?"

"Big cats, much bigger than you, very quick with long front legs to reach into our holes."

The pups fell silent and huddled together by the pond. In the quiet, Cecil thought about what Willy had told him and Anton about another kind of dog out here.

"What about . . . coyotes?" he asked.

The prairie pups squeezed their eyes shut and shivered; Cecil heard one of them whimper and sigh.

"They are the worst of our enemies," Jojo answered quietly. "They come at night in packs, endlessly patient and ruthless. We've lost many friends and family to those fiends."

Cecil sat up and glanced over his shoulder at the sun, now low on the horizon. Jojo read his thoughts. "You should stay with us tonight, to be safe," he said.

Cecil regarded the mounds warily, hesitating. "Underground?"

"Better than above, Cecil, small cat from the ocean," replied Jojo, herding the pups back to their holes. "Better than above."

✣ ✣ ✣

The night passed slowly and was unlike any Cecil had ever spent on land or sea. Stuffed into one of the prairie dog tunnels—though not so far that he couldn't stretch his neck and still glimpse the stars in the blue-black sky above—he squirmed, trying to get comfortable in the shifting dirt. *This is ridiculous!* he thought miserably. *No self-respecting cat should be crammed into an underground dog burrow.* After several hours of restless dozing, he decided to crawl out for a breath of fresh air, despite Jojo's repeated warnings about staying inside. He'd just begun to wriggle his bulk toward the opening when he heard a chilling sound. A howl, long and sharp-edged, not far away. Joined by another, rising and falling in an eerie tone, mournful but eager at the same time.

Could it be them? wondered Cecil, his fur on end. *Coyotes?* He shrank back and listened intently. After a time there came pawsteps from something bigger than Cecil, and there was more than one. He heard them trot past the mounds and circle back, stopping and sniffing, panting. The beasts gave off a pungent, musty scent, dry and stinging to Cecil's nose. They barked to one another; he couldn't quite make out the words but they sounded cruel, ugly.

A shadow fell across Cecil's hole and he held his breath, motionless. In the moonlight he saw a large-eared sharp face, like a dog's but wilder. Its mouth was full of spiked teeth, and its black-rimmed yellow eyes searched the darkness. Cecil's heart stuttered—this *must* be a coyote. The passage was too tight for Cecil to back up farther, so he shut his eyes and hoped that his black fur looked like emptiness.

And it might have, except for one thing.

"Whiskers!" snarled the coyote to the others. "White whiskers plain as day." It leaned into the hole, its tongue flicking across its black lips.

Cecil quickly turned his face into his paws but he knew it was too late. The coyote growled and then drove its snout straight at him, snapping its jagged teeth in the tunnel inches from Cecil's head. The creature scrabbled furiously with its paws to widen the opening. Cecil was trapped, the smooth tunnel walls squeezing him on all sides. He

pulled into a tight ball as clods of dirt rolled down around him. The coyote's yelps knifed through the small space and Cecil flattened his ears against his head. A splat of vile drool hit one ear and he shuddered. He could feel the warmth and meaty stink of the creature's breath as it inched closer, and he cringed and shook and wished he'd had time to say goodbye to Anton. Would he ever see his careful, quiet brother again?

At that moment Cecil felt the oddest sensation on the opposite end of him: his tail was being pulled, pulled *hard,* by sharp little claws. He lifted one ear and thought he heard wild shrieks farther down the tunnel, muffled by his large backside, and then again came the nauseating feeling that his tail might be yanked right *off* his body. Not many things irritated Cecil more than having his tail pulled, and against his better judgment he swiftly uncurled and yowled at the top of his lungs. The coyote jerked away in surprise while at the same time Cecil's hind legs pushed forcefully into the dirt below, causing a small collapse in the tunnel floor. Cecil dropped through like a keg of fish.

He landed on his back, the wind knocked out of him, at the bottom of a large chamber surrounded by dozens of chittering prairie dogs leaping around him in madcap excitement. They prodded him to his feet and hustled him down other passages filled with dusky dirt and squeezy pass-throughs. Cecil lost track of time and distance in the tunnels as they stopped to listen, changed direction and stopped again, then waited in complete darkness for what seemed like hours, all breathing quietly together. Finally they heard the coyotes curse and give up, circling once more and padding away into the night.

Cecil tried to doze again with the inhabitants of prairie dog town nestled all around him, but he couldn't sleep, remembering over and over how close the hot breath and snapping jaws had come. More than that, he lay awake marveling at how, once the tunnel collapsed, the coyote hadn't followed.

He smiled weakly in the dark. Thank the stars and the Great Cats above, the coyote hadn't followed.

❖ ❖ ❖

"They don't like to come in very far, that's a fact," said Jojo, standing with Cecil in the warm sunlight the next morning, supervising the reconstruction of the demolished mound entrance. "They worry that they might become trapped, or ambushed, I suppose." He looked sidelong at Cecil. "Still, you were lucky."

Cecil nodded slowly, feeling more grateful than lucky. "If you all hadn't pulled me down . . ."

Jojo cut in, waving a paw and smiling. "Just go on and find your brother, all right? Family is important." Several of the pups scampered over to Cecil and began petting and grooming his coarse fur, still gritty from the night's escapades.

Yes, and I'd better get a move on if I'm to make any progress, Cecil thought. But the idea of leaving this boisterous group behind and walking alone down the rail line all day was disagreeable and, worse, what if night fell again before he reached the next stop? How would he defend himself against coyotes and other still unknown things that ate cats?

Jojo started to say something else, but suddenly looked down at the ground and then out across the prairie grasses, his eyes narrowed. He whirled to face the mounds, lifted his nose straight up, and began calling loudly and urgently, two long yelps followed by two short yaps. The whole community froze for a moment, sitting tall on their hind legs to listen, then dashed madly for the tunnel openings.

A few of the larger prairie dogs repeated Jojo's call and scurried to herd the pups in before following.

"What is it?" called Cecil. "Coyotes?"

"No!" replied Jojo, headed for a hole. "But we have to get out of the way! Come on!" In a flash he disappeared into the mounds.

And in seconds Cecil was entirely alone, standing outside the prairie dog town in confusion. That's when he felt it in his paws: a deep rumbling in the earth, shaking steadily and growing in intensity. It could have been a train approaching, but the sound wasn't coming from the tracks. He looked at the holes in the dirt and his stomach turned over—he couldn't go back down there in those close, airless corridors, not so soon after getting out.

He looked around wildly and spied a lone pine tree near a rocky outcropping. Dashing to it in long strides, he leaped to the trunk, his claws gripping the bark expertly, and took five or six bounding jumps straight up until he found a thick branch to climb out on. There he crouched, clinging tightly. His heart thumping in his chest, Cecil surveyed the ground but saw nothing. He gazed out over the prairie dog town, past the rock piles and above the fields of swaying grasses, and finally he saw them in the distance. An enormous herd, huge and horned, moving at incredible speed and kicking up great clouds of dust with immense heavy hooves. They overspread the fields like dark running water, the prairie dog town directly in their path.

Cecil had no idea what they were, but he really hoped that they could not climb trees.

CHAPTER 8

One Moonlit Night

Anton heard Cecil's shout and then the murmur among the human passengers who sounded amused by what they had just seen. His heart sank and he pressed his back close to the trembling wall of the carriage as the train picked up speed. They were not, evidently, about to arrive at the next stop. Anton thought that Cecil had probably survived the expulsion; he was good at falling into and out of trouble. He recalled his brother's tale of swinging on a rope from one ship to another with a little bag containing a valuable stone clamped in his jaws. But even if Cecil was fine, how would he manage to get to the next stop? He wouldn't have trouble finding it—just follow the tracks—but suppose it took days and there was nothing to eat?

Anton longed to get out from under the seat and look out the window, just to have some idea what was going by. Was it towns or just the end-less fields of grass they'd seen in the early stages of their journey? He reasoned that it might not be a good idea to get himself thrown off as well, es-pecially as the train seemed to be moving from a pleasant jogging trot to a full-out gallop. The whis-tle blew, the walls vibrated, and the rattling of the metal connections between the carriages sounded like they might just come apart. Anton closed his eyes tight, made himself as small as he could, and waited for whatever came next. He hoped the train stopped someplace with food and not so many hot, jostling, constantly talking humans.

He dozed, his tongue out, the pads of his paws sweating from the heat, and when he woke it was because the passengers were moving about, tak-ing down their hats and jackets from the hooks overhead, milling in the aisles and exchanging pleasantries. They sounded as eager as Anton was, stuck under a bench, for this train to arrive at a destination. When the whistle blew, the train began to slow down and the door at the end of the carriage was thrown open by a man who shouted something. *Yes,* Anton thought. *This is it.* Just wait until all the passengers were out and then make a dash for it.

It didn't take long before the boxes and bags had been hauled away and the last boots had exited at the end of the car. Anton ran to the doorway using the benches for cover, his senses alert to determine which way to turn for the nearest shelter. The Captain was standing on the planks outside, speaking to a lingering passenger, and didn't even see the small gray streak run back alongside the train, then leap across the track and dash into some low grass on the far side. Once hidden from view, Anton crouched low and looked back at the scene. No one had seen him, and the humans were dispersing, going into the wooden building behind the planks or heading toward a line of horses and carts that were waiting to take them away.

Anton felt relieved to have his paws on solid ground with a thin, hot breeze blowing across his cheeks. Even though his mouth was so dry it felt like sand, he took a moment to wipe his face and ears to get the smell of the train out of his nose. Train travel was definitely not his preferred way to get anywhere.

The situation looked promising—lots of places to hide, the smell of food coming from a building across the tracks, and a long trough where a couple of horses stood sucking in water in that odd way they had of drinking. A number of buildings crouched together along the road, and beyond them a few more with wide yards and thin trees leaning over them. Dogs were all over the place, barking at one another, scratching and lounging in whatever shade they could find. In the other direction was grass, grass, and more grass, with a few trees scattered here and there. It wasn't Lunenburg, where he could pass an evening listening to the sailors singing in the saloon or have a chat with old Billy about times gone by, but it was a town of sorts.

Anton darted back across the tracks and crept along the building until he was close enough to the horse trough to observe that it was leaking water at one end, making a nice puddle for drinking. He moved swift and low until he was under the trough and had a good long drink, his ears scanning back and forth for sounds of danger. Music and laughter issued from one building with a long awning across the front, but the songs were unfamiliar and the instruments strange; he couldn't make head nor tail of it. Still, he crouched by the corner for a long while, listening to the crooning, feeling melancholy in the strange town.

His next mission, finding something to eat, was quickly accomplished when he observed a man come out of a side door to dump a bucket of scraps into an uncovered bin. After cautiously looking about in all directions, Anton made a dash across the dirt road and leaped right into the bin. He had his choice of cheesy bits, cut-up meats, and something white and pasty, but not in a bad way. No fish, but one couldn't be finicky while traveling. As he ate he recalled the mountains of fish dumped on the wharf in his home town, glistening and flipping about, easy to cadge and delicious to eat. What was he doing in this place where there was more grass than water?

Anton finished his meal and leaped back out of the bin. He heard the shouts of the conductor, the sliding of doors and bustle of people getting back on, then the whistle tore through the air. Anton could never hear it without a moment of sheer terror. He stood his ground, but sank down on his haunches. The train pulled slowly away from the platform, heading for the sun, which was low now, sliding into a sky streaked with red and green. When the last car was well away, Anton crossed the tracks again without hurrying. There was no one around. He figured he would sleep in the grass so he wouldn't miss the next train, on which, hopefully, his brother would have somehow caught a ride.

The grass was well over his head. With a little patting and tramping, he made a good hiding place, comfortable if a little prickly. It was a warm, clear evening and the stars were switching on as the light faded. He stretched out, resting his chin on his paws. *Cecil,* he thought. *The big oaf.* He was never much good at hiding.

"S'cuse me," a voice said from somewhere in the grass.

Anton opened his eyes wide, without lifting his head. It was dark now, and late from the feel of the air. He had been deep in sleep, and for a moment he thought what he'd heard was just the rustling of the grass. There was a whisper of a breeze, but then the voice, which had a squeaky, oily quality about it, repeated, "S'cuse me." The grasses just ahead of Anton's face parted and a black nose poked through.

Anton drew his head back but still didn't move. "You're excused," he said.

The nose twitched and there was a chuckling sound, then the rest of a small pointed face with black masked eyes, light cheeks, and pointed ears appeared. "Hey," said the face. "Are you funnin' me?"

For want of anything better to say, Anton replied, "My name is Anton."

"Anton," the creature said. "Howdy. Howdy do."

It was like listening to humans, Anton thought. You had an idea what they meant sometimes, but you could never be sure. The creature emerged entirely now and sat down, staring with his beady eyes, patting his full belly, cleaning his sharp cat-like teeth with the pointed end of a long stalk of grass. But he wasn't a cat, Anton was sure of that. He had a low, slinky, tan body and a bushy tail with a black tip. His shoulders, legs, and feet were black and his paws were definitely not cat paws. His neck was too long; also his head was too small.

He was larger than Anton by half, but he had a daffy look about him that wasn't threatening. Suddenly whatever he was leaped straight up in the air and came down on the other side of Anton, disappearing briefly into the grass. Then he reappeared, his head emerging and sinking again, his back arched, then stretching out long, tearing through the grass in a wide circle until he came back and took his seat.

"You wanna play?" he asked.

"I don't think so," Anton said.

"Aw, come on. You chase me, then I chase you."

It occurred to Anton that if he chased this silly animal, he would be able to catch him, and then where would they be? "I'm too tired," he said. "I've been traveling on the train and I have to wait here for my brother."

"Gotcha," said the creature. "That's my name. Gotcha. Ain't that a scream?"

Anton smiled. It was a funny name. "I take it you're from around here."

"Sure," said Gotcha. "My family lives over yonder. I got a brother, too, and two sisters. Momma died last year."

"I'm sorry to hear that. Please accept my sympathy."

"Thankee kindly," said Gotcha. "Momma was one fine ferret. Nothing she couldn't find if'n she wanted to find it." Anton noticed that the ferret's eyes squinted a little, and he sniffed. But then he shook his head and swallowed hard. "I know yer some kind of a cat," he said. "But yer not very big."

Anton drew himself up at that. "I'm not that small."

"Compared to the cats we have around here, yer just a little sprout. They're bigger'n you when they get born."

"How big do they get?"

"You want to see some of 'em? There's a family over yonder up that hill."

"No thanks. I want to stay close to the tracks because I think my brother will be on the next train."

"Well, that might be tomorry night and it might be the next, but it surely won't be tonight. They don't come through here but once't every coupla days."

"You're sure about that?"

"Sure as shootin'," replied Gotcha.

"Well . . ." said Anton.

"Come on along," said Gotcha. "You'll be right

tickled to see the big baby cats. They're just startin' to try to hunt a little, chas'n' crickets and like that. They're mighty cute now, though they won't be when they git growed."

Anton looked toward the hills. He felt wide awake now and curious about this place with its strange inhabitants. If no train was coming any-time soon, he might as well check out the sights. Gotcha seemed an amiable sort of fellow, as goofy as Cecil and just as eager for some fun. And he clearly knew his way around, so Anton would have no trouble finding his way back to the tracks.

"Okay," Anton said. "You lead the way."

"Catch me if you can," Gotcha squeaked, and took off through the grass, flattening it like a wagon wheel. Anton raced in his tracks—it was easy enough. The ferret had a loping gait because he was so long, and though he was pretty fast, Anton could easily have passed him. It felt great to race through the night after days of being cooped up in the train carriages. The moon was fading and the grasses hummed with those crickets the youngsters were doubtless chasing. Anton thought of his little brother Clive, who was almost grown now but still idolized Cecil and would sit and listen to his exaggerated sea tales for hours on end. The grasses thinned, and there was a slow rise to chalkier soil. Before a line of ragged-looking trees, Gotcha slowed to a trot and Anton drew up beside him, breathing in the warm night air.

"They play over by that little stream," he said. "The momma goes out hunting and leaves them there. They don't wander far. They know she's strict about that."

Anton perked up as they approached the cracked mud banks of the stream. "Any fish in there?" he asked.

"Not much. Frogs though. The tadpoles ain't bad eatin', but I don't like 'em once't they get legs."

Anton nodded. He completely agreed with this assessment of amphibians as food items.

Standing on his hind legs and looking in all directions, Gotcha stretched his long neck and body up, his forelegs dropped at his sides. He was quite tall, Anton noticed. He could probably see right over that grass when he stood like that.

"I see 'em," Gotcha said. "Right down on that bank." He gave Anton a sidelong glance. "We best be careful now. We might not want to be hangin' round her babies when that Momma comes down from the mountain, know what I mean? She could up and lose her temper if she sees us too close to 'em."

Anton smiled. "How big is she?" he asked.

"You'd be about two bites, I'd say."

Anton followed as Gotcha ambled along. They could hear the cubs now, making low mewing sounds and fake roars. As they descended the bank Anton saw them, and it was true—they were enormous light tan kittens covered with dark spots. They had striped foreheads and bobbed tails, and oversized furry, pointy ears. One was crouched, prepared to attack something in the water, and the other was teetering on a large stone, looking down on his brother and about to pounce upon his back.

"Lookit," said Gotcha, as the brother cubs sprang at once and wound up rolling together into the shallow water. "I remember when I used to play like that with my brother."

"Me, too," said Anton.

The cubs had scrambled out of the water and were chasing each other back up the bank. "Watch out, watch out," said one.

"You can't get me," said the other. They weren't looking where they were going and had to dodge rocks and tree trunks on the fly. They were heading straight for their audience of cat and ferret. Anton looked on, much entertained, but as the cubs came together and play-attacked each other, rolling in a furry ball of tails, heads, and paws in the dirt, Anton spotted something just beyond that made him catch his breath.

It was a large snake, its body coiled, its head raised, watching the cubs coldly as they drew closer and closer.

Gotcha saw it, too. "It's a durned rattler," he whispered. No sooner had he said this than a strange shaking sound, like nothing Anton had ever heard, rose from the reptile's body. The sound made Anton bare his teeth and hiss.

Gotcha's mouth squinched up in a knot and he leaned forward on his black paws. "We got to do somethin', Anton, or those cubs is done for. You take the back, I'll get the front," he said. "Just get a grip and pull."

"Gotcha," said Anton. And it was not until they were both streaking into the clearing that he realized he'd said the ferret's name.

The cubs looked up from their play to see a very small cat and a large ferret covering ground like two lightning bolts. They backed away, letting out high-pitched cries of alarm.

The snake never knew what was coming. Gotcha dove onto the reptile's head from behind, and as the scaly body uncoiled, Anton caught the other end and bit hard, pulling back with all his strength. When the snake was stretched out between them, Gotcha released its head and the long body rose high in the air. Anton leaped back, turning his head to one side, and let go of the tail. The snake sailed through the air, unable to coil itself, and came down with a crack against a rocky outcropping, where it paused for only a moment before slithering with surprising speed in the opposite direction.

"Holy Mo," said Gotcha. "That's the first time I seen a snake fly."

The cubs came running then, shouting to their rescuers. "You saved us, you saved us! He was going to bite my brother. Momma said those rattlers are so dangerous. You saved us! Wait till we tell Momma." As they calmed down and had a good look at Anton and Gotcha, their eyes grew wide.

"What are you?" the bigger one said to Anton. "Are you some kind of ferret?"

"I'm a cat. I'm not from around here. My name is Anton."

"Oh," said the cub, leaning against his brother's side. "We're sort of cats, too, I think. Lynxes, Momma says."

Gotcha looked on, clearly pleased with himself. "I'm Mr. Gotcha," he said. "You tell your momma it was me and Mr. Anton here what watched over you while you was waitin' on her."

"We'll tell her," they said together. "She'll be back soon."

Gotcha gave Anton a look of mild alarm. "We best be goin', right, Mr. Anton?"

Anton took the hint. "Right, Mr. Gotcha," he said. "You kits be careful now."

At that moment a ferocious scream rang out in the distance. Anton's fur stood along his spine. In the cloudy moonlight he made out the figure of a creature, cat-like but three times as big as he was, topping a rocky rise and streaking toward them with alarming speed.

"Is that . . . ?" Anton began.

"That's the momma," cried Gotcha. "Run, Mr. Anton!"

The pair sprang away from the cubs and raced

across the clearing toward the tall grass beyond the stream. Anton had always thought of himself as a fast runner, but the momma lynx closed the distance in seconds. She snarled furiously, almost on top of them as they burst into the line of grass. Gotcha ran a few yards behind, and Anton heard the snap of jaws and a yip from the ferret as they scrambled blindly through the brush.

"Gotcha!" called Anton as he ran. "You okay?"

"Still here!" panted Gotcha from somewhere nearby. "But we ain't gonna outrun her, Anton."

"Head for the tracks!" yelled Anton, hoping that the human buildings and smells would turn the lynx away. They swerved and the train station loomed ahead, and at last the sounds of pursuit faded. The mother lynx had let them go. They stopped near some spindly shrubs, leaning to catch their breath.

"Whoo-ee, that was right close," said Gotcha, examining his backside where the lynx had grazed him with her teeth.

"Too close," said Anton, shaking his head, though the sight of the huge wild cat had been briefly thrilling.

"Never underestimate a momma," said Gotcha.

"My own was tough as nails, just like that, always protectin' her kits."

Anton nodded, thinking of Sonya far away across the land and sea, taking care of his little brothers and sisters. He wondered if she'd be surprised to hear that her sons had managed to lose each other in a strange world, once again.

CHAPTER 9

Wild Ride

The prairie dogs came out of their mounds long before Cecil was willing to climb down from the tree.

"Come on!" called Jojo, sitting on his hind legs and peering up at Cecil. "It's fine!"

Doesn't look fine to me, Cecil thought, still clinging to the branch. The herd of animals had poured across the plain in enormous numbers, their hooves pounding the grasses flat as they came, running roughshod over rocks and shrubs and even the prairie dog holes until finally slowing to a booming trot. The front edge of the herd crowded around the pond, slurping noisily, and Cecil had a good view of the monstrous beasts.

He'd seen cows and he'd seen horses, but these were bigger than either—wide bodies covered in shaggy brown coats, tall as a human at the shoulders, with split hooves that could crush a cat. But the oddest thing about them was their heads. Long and bearded, with pointed horns on top and wide black nostrils near the bottom, their giant faces looked vaguely skeptical, mostly because of the camouflaged brown eyes on either side, half-closed, reserved.

From his tree perch, the herd filled Cecil's vision like a dark ocean before him, rippling as the creatures grazed and scuffled. *How will I get out of here?* he wondered. But the prairie dogs had ventured from their holes as soon as the stampeding had ended, resuming their tasks as if there were no hulking creatures strolling nearby.

Jojo tried again. "Seriously, Cecil, come down." He gestured with a paw. "They're called *bison,* and they don't eat us. You just have to keep out from underhoof."

If the bison were curious about why Jojo was yelling, they didn't show it—none even glanced

Cecil's way. Cecil sighed and began to climb slowly down the tree trunk, tail first. At the bottom he paused and then slunk quickly between the me-andering beasts to the prairie dog town. Jojo was in the middle of things, helping with the repairs, showing the pups how to shore up the tunnels once again. The pups were more interested in playing, some riding on others' backs over the mounds and squeaking joyfully, *Yee ha!*

Cecil sat nearby, cleaning sticky sap off of his fur, and watched the lumbering bison take huge mouthfuls of grass, chew patiently, and swallow it down. *Maybe not cat eaters,* he thought, *though probably cat stompers.* He gazed toward the rails in the distance and saw a straight open line like a vein through the throng—the big brutes seemed to avoid the train rails altogether.

"I guess I should get going," Cecil said to Jojo. "I'll stay on the tracks when I walk."

The prairie dog yipped instructions to the pups and turned to Cecil. "You ought to talk to some of the bison before you go," he said, pulling Cecil to one side as a small calf, still bigger than they were, scampered past.

"Talk to them?" asked Cecil. "Why?"

"They travel far and wide, move across the plains quickly when they want to. They see a lot—maybe they'd know something about your brother."

"But . . ." Cecil hesitated, looking up at the huge horned faces.

Jojo smiled. "They're nicer than they look. Kind of quiet, though. They are beasts of very few words."

"Hmmm," said Cecil. He was doubtful, but he spotted two or three bison grazing a little apart from the herd and carefully made his way toward them.

"Hello," Cecil said as he approached. The bison continued chewing. Cecil stepped around to face the largest one directly and looked up at its massive hairy head.

"Hi, my name is Cecil," he tried again, a little louder.

The bison stopped chewing and fixed his mud-colored eyes on Cecil.

"Skunk," it said flatly. Its deep voice thudded like a ship's hull hitting rocks.

Cecil shook his head. "No, I'm not a skunk. I'm a cat."

The bison snorted, sending up dust. "Skunk."

"I'm a . . . a *small* cat, and I'm traveling to find my brother Anton, who is gray and even smaller than me." *This is hopeless,* Cecil thought. "What's your name?"

The bison ripped up a strip of prairie grass and chewed it slowly. "Dirk," he said finally. The two bison on either side of him swung their heads in Cecil's direction as if the question had been meant for them as well.

"Hank," said one.

"Chuck," said the other.

"Pleased to meet you all," said Cecil politely. "Do any of you know how far it is to the next town?"

Dirk continued munching on grass and slid his eyes over the prairie, as if considering.

Hank stepped closer—*thud, thud.* "Far," he said.

Cecil sighed. "That's what I thought. I got all the way out here on the train, but now I guess I'll have to walk . . ." He tipped his head toward the tracks on their raised ridge to show what he meant.

Dirk's eyes flew from half-closed to three-quarters open. Chuck stamped one hoof, hard. *Thunk.* Cecil sprang back.

"Pusher!" said Chuck.

"Crusher!" added Hank.

Dirk shook his great head grimly. "Danger."

Cecil looked from one to the other of them, trying to make sense of it. "Do you mean that the train is dangerous?"

The bison all stared at him as if his question was remarkably dumb.

"Do you mean that the train sometimes runs into the bison?" Cecil ventured.

Hank snorted impatiently.

Cecil continued under their glare. "And that's why you stay away from the rails?"

Dirk shifted his considerable weight and leaned toward Cecil. "Bingo."

So they avoid the trains, thought Cecil. *But surely they must know where they go, and how far.* A wild idea began to form in his mind. He remembered how terrifyingly fast they had come in with all the noise, dust, and mayhem. It was chaotic and pulse-quickening, a crazy speeding horde. Jojo had said the bison covered a lot of ground, and Cecil really could use a lift.

"So, Dirk," said Cecil conversationally, sidling up as close as he dared. "When you guys decide to move out again, how about giving me a ride to the next town?"

"Ride?" said Dirk, still huffing from the talk of the train.

"On your back, I mean." Cecil smiled and gave Dirk a wink. "I'm as light as a feather."

Dirk shook his head slowly. "Skunk," he snorted.

"No, I'm a—" began Cecil.

"Stink," Dirk insisted, a little louder.

"I smell fine," Cecil protested, moving closer. "Here, smell me."

Dirk planted his hooves, sending up a plume of dust. "Stay," he warned, and lowered his great head.

Cecil skittered sideways, tail up and ears pricked. "Okay, okay!" he said quickly. "No ride, I get it." He backed up a few more feet to a safe distance and sat down cautiously, eyeing Dirk's sharp horns. Bison were quirky, and he sure didn't want to be in the path of an angry one.

The bison seemed to lose interest in Cecil and moved toward fresh patches of grass. Dirk stepped over to a shallow, dusty spot in the ground, bent his knees and tipped over into the dirt—*whump*. He rolled on his back from side to side, grinding the dirt into his shaggy coat and kicking his hooves in the air.

Cecil was startled by the sheer energy of the maneuver. "What's he doing?" he asked Chuck.

Chuck looked over. "Itchy," he said.

Of course, Cecil thought. *I do that myself some-times. Though not in the dirt. It'll take him hours to clean that.* Cecil eyed Dirk's coat with distaste, and then another idea took hold. *Itchy, huh? Skunk my whiskers. I'll show him what a feline can do.* He walked closer to the wallowing Dirk and waited until the beast paused on one huge side, his eye rolling skyward. Cecil moved around behind him, popped out his claws, and, stretching up on his back legs, carefully placed his front paws on Dirk's back and began to scratch.

Dirk's enormous torso stiffened for a moment, and Cecil tensed to spring away if the beast sud-denly rolled toward him. But Dirk relaxed against the ground. The bison closed his eyes and made deep chuffing sounds that Cecil could feel under his paws, like a purring kitten the size of a horse-cart. Cecil padded and scratched the shaggy ex-panse until he grew tired, and then sat back. Dirk rolled up to standing and gazed at Cecil with new-found admiration.

"Cat!" he said.

Cecil nodded and shook some of the dust from his own fur. "Cat. You got it." He waited for Dirk's appreciation to turn into an offer of help, but the bison continued to stare at him blankly, the hair of his beard tossing in the prairie wind.

Cecil sighed. "Well this has been great fun," he said, standing to go. "But I'll be taking my leave of you fine fellows now."

Hank and Chuck nodded in a leisurely way, tearing more bunches of prairie grass up by the roots, but Dirk shifted his stance—*thud, thud*—to face Cecil. "Leave," Dirk said heavily. Behind him the herd undulated gently, swelling and curling along the far edges.

"Yep," said Cecil, edging back a few paces. His plan to charm his way into a ride had gone nowhere, and now the bison were actually telling him to get out. *I must be losing my touch,* he thought glumly.

Dirk raised his mammoth head high into the breeze, looking, it seemed to Cecil, in the direction of the setting sun. "Go," he said, and snorted once.

"I'm going, all right?" *Great cats,* thought Cecil, *he can't get rid of me soon enough.* "I'm gone." He turned and trotted off, weaving carefully between the bison, who seemed to have begun to stroll in the same direction and all together. He was past the pond and headed for the rails when he heard a determined plonking behind him, and turned to find Dirk following in his path. Cecil's heart jumped in his chest—was the bison chasing him now? Behind Dirk the herd was beginning to flow, the center middle surging ahead while the flanks curved away behind, all of the animals picking up speed.

Dirk reached Cecil and loomed over him. "Cat!" he boomed.

"Yes?" Cecil cringed in the creature's shadow.

"Go!" Dirk rumbled.

"I'm trying to!" said Cecil, exasperated.

"Ride!" said Dirk. He turned toward the herd and took a step or two, then glanced back.

Cecil's mouth hung open. Was Dirk really offering a ride? "You mean it?" He looked at Dirk's mellow brown eyes, calm and dignified beneath his curved, pointy horns.

Dirk raised one back hoof and brought it down hard. *Stomp.* "Now," he said.

Cecil jumped. "Of course!" he spluttered. "Right, let's go!" With a leaping bound he pulled himself up to Dirk's back and forward to the hump above his shoulders. He flattened down and held on. Dirk took a couple of trotting steps and then launched into a canter, all muscle and power as he joined his fellow bison, swerving and jostling in the fray. Cecil dug in with his claws to stay on, squinting through the billowing dust.

"Ouch," said Dirk evenly.

"Sorry!" shouted Cecil. He loosened his grip slightly, but only slightly, as all around Dirk ran thundering bison, large and small. Dirt was already in Cecil's mouth and eyes, but soon he got a feel for the rolling motion and relaxed a little. This was faster than a ship, maybe faster than the train. It was certainly more exciting than both, and possibly the most dangerous ride of them all. One slip and he'd be crushed under the stampeding hooves. He didn't know when they'd stop or how he'd get off, but he would worry about that later.

For now he was Cecil, small cat from the ocean, riding across the plains on the back of a bison. *Yee ha!*

✤ ✤ ✤

As Anton and Gotcha made their way back across the deep grass, the stars faded overhead and the sky paled. Gotcha yawned once, then again,

opening his black mouth wide and showing all his sharp teeth. "It's gettin' on to my bedtime," he said. "I'll see you back to them tracks and head for the sack."

"I'm feeling sleepy myself," Anton admitted. "But I'm glad I took a look around. This is a strange world you live in."

"Don't seem funny to me, but then I never been anywheres else."

"I guess I'll just sleep in the grass here by this field," Anton said. "That way I'll hear the train."

"I wouldn't do that if I was you," Gotcha said. "Sometimes all manner of animals are about, and yer so small you could get stepped on or mistaken for a meal. Sometimes bison come running through here, fast as the train, and you don't get no warning. I almost got kilt once, 'cause I stopped to watch 'em and one split off and near run me down."

"What are bison?"

"Bison? Hard to say. They've got hooves but they're not horses or cows. They're bigger for one thing. Big furry fellers, with beards. They don't talk much and every now and then they take it into their heads to herd up and run as fast as they can."

Anton nodded. "You're right. That sounds

dangerous." They were approaching the wooden building. It was nearly dawn and no one, man or beast, was out and about except for the small gray cat and his new friend the ferret. Anton noticed a ladder leaning at one end of the building, leading up to the flat porch roof that extended over the platform. "That looks like a safe bet," he said.

"What's that?"

"I can run up that ladder and sleep on the roof. Then I'll be able to see everything and nothing will see me."

"That's a durned good idea. You're as smart as they come," said Gotcha. "I never seen an animal with wits like you got. It's no surprise yer out here where you never been before."

But Anton was thinking that it was very surprising he was here. For a moment he had to remind himself how he'd gotten this far from home and why. He didn't enjoy adventure the way Cecil did, but it was interesting how different one place was from another. Gotcha said good night, though it was morning, and slunk off into the grass, heading for his burrow in the low brush at the foot of the hills. Anton watched him until he was out of sight and then leaped up the ladder and strolled along the roof looking out at the view. It was a pleasant enough sleeping spot, with a light breeze cooling the air. And it was perfectly safe, as no one on the ground could see him unless he approached the edges. He curled up near the back wall, thinking about the oversized kittens. How huge their mother was. How awkward and funny they were— like Clive when he was just learning to hunt. And thinking of kittens, Anton drifted into a deep sleep.

When he woke the sun was blazing into his eyes and the tin roof beneath his paws was heating up fast. Stranger still was the sense he had that it was moving, not just the roof, but the whole building, the whole world. There was a pulsing in the air and a sound, distant but definitely coming closer, like rolling thunder in the midst of a storm. Could the train be coming in? Anton got up to have a look down the track. There was a cloud of some sort, well past the track and wider than any train could produce. It looked as though the grass must be on fire, burning a wide swath and sending up a steady current of pale brown smoke.

The sound grew more intense and made the fur on Anton's neck stand up. He crouched low and saw that there was something under the cloud, something with many, many hooves. It was just as Gotcha had warned him, and as the herd approached, Anton was heartily thankful he hadn't gone to sleep in the grass. The bison were coming at a breakneck pace. In a few moments, Anton made out the animals in the front, their huge brown heads lowered, their hooves driving in relentless unison. Soon they were passing the station and he could see them clearly, their humped-up backs and shaggy coats. It was quite a show, and Anton had a very good seat. For what seemed a long time the bison herd roared onward, rank on rank, like waves rolling against the side of a ship. At last they thinned out a bit, the slower animals, perhaps the oldest and the youngest, bringing up the rear. Anton noticed something odd about one bison in particular—he was running hard, just like the others, but he held his back oddly. Then Anton realized that it wasn't his back but something *on* his back. Something black and furry. Something with a tail. Anton stood up high on his toes, riveted to the sight.

Then he let out a cry. *CECIL?*

It was Cecil, riding on the back of a furiously galloping bison.

CECIL! Anton felt his heart racing with fear. What could he do? Then, as Anton stood helplessly watching, a small bison running next to the one carrying Cecil missed a step and came down hard on his side, knocking into the heels of Cecil's bison and causing it to lurch. Cecil was thrown free of his mount—Anton saw his brother spring up, and fall down, out of sight. The downed bison staggered to his feet, snorting and stamping, then, without looking back, lumbered on to catch up with his fellows. Anton rushed to the ladder and sprinted down to the ground. Keeping one eye on the receding herd and the other on the spot where he had seen his brother fall, he dashed into the grass.

The grass was deep just beyond the tracks, but Anton pushed through it and then it flattened out before him, a wide plain, hammered to damp mush by the furious hooves of the bison. In the midst of it he could see Cecil, lying on his side, not moving. Terror struck him and he called out, "Cecil!"

Cecil lifted his head, then dropped it back down again with a yowl of pain.

He's hurt, thought Anton, breaking into a run. *Oh, why did we come out to this crazy place?*

By the time Anton reached his brother's side,

Cecil was trying to sit up, groaning as he did. "Oh, my leg," he said. "Great cats, that hurts."

"What did you do?" Anton said, bumping noses and passing a paw over Cecil's shoulder.

"It's my back leg. I'm afraid to look at it." He shifted his weight and rolled back down, exposing the leg he'd landed on.

Anton let out a gasp. The flesh was torn from Cecil's hip to his hock and the wound was bleeding profusely. "This is terrible," he said. "What are we going to do?"

At that moment, they heard a high-pitched shout and looked up to see a large cat-like creature barreling toward them across the matted grass at high speed.

"Are you all right?" the animal called as it came to a skidding halt before the startled brothers. "I saw you fall from over there. You were riding on a bison. I've never seen a sight like that in all my days!"

This cat was three times the size of Cecil. It had large, pointy, tufted ears and a thick, spotted coat, big, plush feet, and, strangest of all, a short, stiff-looking tail. *Just like those baby lynxes I saw with Gotcha,* Anton thought nervously.

"You're the tiniest cats I've ever seen," the marvelous-looking creature remarked. It gazed at Anton for a moment. "You're Anton, aren't you?"

Anton's mouth went dry. Was this the momma lynx? Would she still be angry about the cubs? Anton tried to shift attention to his brother. "Yes. And this is Cecil. He's hurt."

"I'm Katya," the cat said. "My sister told me that you saved her cubs from a rattler, and I'm very grateful. Perhaps I can return the favor." Anton let out a small sigh of relief, nodding politely to her and ignoring Cecil's questioning glance.

Katya stepped over to look at Cecil's leg. "I'm not surprised you're injured," she said. "That was quite a fall. Can you stand up?"

"I'll give it a try," Cecil said, and he pulled himself, groaning, to his feet.

"Try taking just a few steps," Katya said.

Anton felt his throat tighten. Something about Katya reminded him of his mother, Sonya. She seemed to know just what to do.

Cecil took one or two steps, then sat down. "I can walk," he said. "But it sure hurts."

"It's not broken," Katya concluded. "But you've lost a lot of blood, so you're very weak."

"This is awful!" Anton exclaimed.

"Are you his friend?" she asked Anton.

"I'm his brother. We came out here on the train and we don't know a soul. What can we do?"

Katya stared at Anton. "You rode the black screamer? Goodness." She looked from him to Cecil. "Do you know much about humans?"

Cecil nodded. "A little. We knew some nice ones and some not so nice where we came from."

"Well, it's the same here. There are some that I know about who might help Cecil. They move around a lot, but they spend summers just beyond that line of trees over there." Katya pointed and the brothers looked at each other. It wasn't too far, and it was flat all the way. "You can lean on your brother and we'll go slowly. There's water there, too."

"How do you know they'll help us?" Cecil asked.

"When I was young, I got hurt pretty badly, and one of them found me nearly dead. He was just a child, but he took good care of me and had some medicine that healed me fast. I'm not afraid of them and they respect me, so if I go with you, I think they'll bind up Cecil's wound and stop the bleeding."

Cecil took a few steps with his head hung low, leaning heavily against Anton.

"That's a brave fellow," Katya said, and she came up on his other side. Between them Anton and Katya supported Cecil and they began a slow progress across the field. Katya glanced once more at the brothers. "One rides in on a train, the other on a bison," she marveled, smiling. "You give cats a good name."

CHAPTER 10

Whale Out of Water

ut on the plains in the midday sun, the air began to heat and thicken. The pace of the three cats, two small and one large, was painfully slow. As Cecil limped alongside, Anton couldn't resist asking him how he'd come to be on the back of a bison.

Cecil shrugged a little. "I needed a ride," he said simply. "It was a long way over here."

Katya chuckled while Anton pressed further. "But they're so huge! Weren't you afraid?"

Cecil considered this. "Nope. After the coyotes,

the bison were no big deal." He didn't mention hiding up in the tree when the herd first stormed in.

"The coyotes?" cried Anton, turning to his brother.

"Mmm-hmmm," said Cecil as he hopped on his good back leg, wincing a bit. "I met one face-to-face, and I can say for sure that I don't ever want to meet another."

Katya nodded and clucked her tongue. "Amen to that. You're lucky you got away. Not many do."

Anton's mouth still hung open. "How *did* you get away?"

"Funny story," said Cecil, grinning at the memory. "Actually, it was the prairie dogs who saved me."

"Dogs?" gasped Anton. "There were dogs out there? Like Willy?"

"Not exactly. I'll fill you in later, and I want to hear about that rattler, too." Cecil gave his brother a wink as they finally neared the line of trees.

Moving carefully through the grove, the cats emerged into a field and stopped to take in the sight. It was a village, busy with humans and animals moving about, but not like any village Anton and Cecil had ever seen. The houses were tall and narrow like the lighthouse back home, but these were made of long branches tilted together at the top and wrapped in large folds of what looked like sailcloth. The humans had straight black fur on their heads that was tied into thick bunches with cords, and they wore flowing clothes and soft shoes. The cats spotted horses, chickens, and goats in penned areas. Dogs and lots of younger humans ran around loose, and tiny faces peeked out of blankets as they were carried on the backs of others who were full-grown.

"Are you sure about this, Katya?" asked Anton, eyeing all of the commotion. "I don't see any other cats in this place."

"Cats here are wild, not penned like these creatures," explained Katya. "Sometimes the humans help us, and in return we don't hurt them, and that's enough for us. Horses and dogs have made a different bargain. They work for the humans and live among them, and in exchange they are assured food and shelter." She turned to Anton. "Okay, stay back for a moment, will you? Come with me, Cecil." She walked slowly, Cecil staggering at her side, toward an open area where a group of young people had formed a circle and were tossing stones at a log in the center. One boy noticed Katya and Cecil and broke from the circle to approach the cats. He pulled a strip of something brown and stiff from his pocket and set it on the ground, then backed up.

Anton watched as Katya stepped forward and took the offering, which smelled salty and smoky, and carried it in her mouth back to Cecil, who snapped it up ravenously. Katya turned, looking at the boy, then moved away from Cecil. The boy caught sight of the blood on Cecil's flank and approached him slowly with another thick strip held out in his hand. *That's certainly the way to my brother's heart,* thought Anton.

All at once Cecil, exhausted and weak from his injury, crumpled to the ground and lay still. Anton gasped, but he could see Cecil's golden eyes were still open and watching Katya. The boy moved carefully to pick Cecil up, and Katya nodded reassuringly to Cecil. The boy carried Cecil in both arms, pressing the bulky cat against his chest, and disappeared into the nearest sailcloth house. Anton's heart squeezed as he stood looking at the closed flap, helpless.

"You're absolutely sure this is okay?" he asked Katya again when she rejoined him.

"I think so," she replied, "though it may take some time."

Anton took a big breath and let it out slowly. *How much time do we have?* he wondered, thinking of Cecil and of Hieronymus, trapped somewhere and in danger.

"You must be hungry," said Katya. "Come on, I know where we can find some tasty lizards."

"Lizards?" said Anton. "To eat?"

"Or mice, if you prefer."

"Mice!" gasped Anton. "Not mice either."

"Goodness, you're particular, aren't you?" said Katya. "Well, beetles, spiders, bats . . . We'll find you something." She turned and trotted away. Anton followed reluctantly. He hated to leave Cecil, but there was nothing to do but wait, and he *was* hungry. He took one last look back at the village where his injured brother was hidden from view, then hurried after the lynx. *Beetles, ugh.*

⚜ ⚜ ⚜

Katya lived in a small cave in the rocky hillside behind the town where the train had come in. She let Anton stay there while he waited for Cecil to recover, and for two days she showed him the ways of this strange new land. Katya hunted at night and Anton closed his eyes and ate whatever she brought back, which he found unsettling. He quickly learned the smells and sounds of the burrowing owls, foxes, and jackrabbits, the rasping scratch of rattlesnakes, and the skittering of scorpions. Late one night as he was drifting to sleep, Anton's ears pricked up to a long soulful howl in the distance. The sound made the fur on his tail stand on end. Katya appeared suddenly from over a nearby rise.

"*That's* a coyote," she called across to him softly. "We'd better head back to the cave."

If a cat as big as Katya is afraid of them, Anton thought, *they must be nasty indeed.*

Each morning the two cats visited the village to look for any sign of Cecil. The boy who had taken him was usually outside with the rest of the smaller humans, but Cecil was not. They assumed he was still inside one of the houses, hopefully on the mend.

On the third morning Katya and Anton approached the village to find everything in motion. Humans doused the fires and packed the cooking tools into bundles, loading them in bags hanging from the sides of horses or onto the carts roped behind them. The men unwrapped the sailcloth from the long branches of the houses and corralled the animals, while the women set the children on horseback or into wagons. Cecil was nowhere to be seen.

"What's happening?" asked Anton, alarmed.

"It's as I told you," said Katya. "They move around a lot, and today must be moving day. Come on, we have to find your brother."

They hurried around the edge of the settlement, trying to avoid being seen while searching for Cecil. Anton worried that he'd already left and was out on the prairie looking for them, or worse— that he had not recovered after all. A panic rose in Anton's belly as he turned every which way in confusion.

"Anton," said Katya anxiously. "I see him."

Anton whirled to find Cecil, up on all four legs and walking without a limp next to the boy who had carried him away. He let out a cry of relief until he saw why Katya sounded concerned. Every few steps Cecil stopped cold, digging into the dirt and twisting his body. Then he was dragged forward again, and Anton saw why. Clutched in the boy's hand was the end of a length of cord that trailed down along his side, the other end tied around Cecil's neck. Anton couldn't believe it—Cecil had been captured by the boy. He was a pet!

"Oh, cat's whiskers!" said Anton.

"I know!" said Katya. "Don't worry, we'll get him."

Cecil and the boy were at the very back of the group now proceeding away from the site, and Anton and Katya sprinted to catch up with them on the dirt path. The boy bent down repeatedly, trying to stroke Cecil's head and speaking softly to him, but Cecil only balked and struggled further. As the boy continued to pull, Cecil flattened himself to the dirt and dug in his claws, scratching along the ground and grasping at any stone or root he could reach. Finally, the boy stopped and sighed. He looked down the path behind Cecil, where Katya and Anton stood a few yards away, staring directly at him. The boy's eyes widened.

Cecil lifted his head, sniffing the air with recognition. "Oh, hey guys!" he called, his voice rough. "Nice of you to show up."

"Are you okay?" asked Anton.

"I've been better," said Cecil, managing a grin despite the cord around his neck. "Katya, please do something about this friend of yours."

"I will," she said, watching the boy, who stood transfixed. "Though I hate to frighten him . . ."

"You hate to frighten *him*?" gasped Cecil. "What about me? I'm tied up like a dog!"

"He *saved* you, remember?" said Katya, frowning. Then she took a breath, bared her pointed teeth, and let out a deep snarl from her chest. Both smaller cats flinched at the sound, and the boy yelped and dropped the cord. Katya's growl instantly caught the attention of some older humans ahead, who turned and yelled, rushing toward them, a few with pointed sticks held high and aimed low.

"Run!" shouted Anton.

"Sorry!" Katya called to the boy.

"And thanks!" yelled Cecil, bounding out of reach.

The three cats flew across the former village site in long, leaping strides, though Cecil lagged a bit due to the trailing cord entangling his paws. At a safe distance, the cats turned to check if they were being followed, but they were not. The villagers watched them go, then continued on with their move to a new part of the prairie, and the cats trotted back to Katya's home in the caves.

❖ ❖ ❖

With Anton and Katya both chewing and pulling, they managed to remove the cord from Cecil's neck. After they'd had a thorough cleaning, plenty of fresh water, and a decent meal, Anton and Cecil lay near the cave entrance looking up at the stars while Katya was out hunting. They told each other the stories of what had happened since they were separated, and then were quiet for a while, each thinking his own thoughts and listening to the night.

"I can see Hunter's Claw from here," said Cecil, pointing a paw at a cluster of stars in the sky. "And Twin Whiskers over there. They're the same whether we're at home or at sea or here."

Anton flicked his tail against the rock. "Maybe. But so much else is different."

"Like, say, the lack of water?" asked Cecil.

"Yes," said Anton, suddenly struck with homesickness. "No ocean. No ships. No sailors. No fish. I really miss all of it."

"Yeah," agreed Cecil. "It's strange out here. I'll give you that."

"And now you've gotten hurt, and we're in constant danger, and we are no closer to finding Hieronymus." Anton let out a slow breath. "I wonder if we should just . . ." He didn't finish.

Cecil turned to look at his brother. "Go home?"

"I don't know," said Anton quietly. "Maybe. Who knows if we can even go back the way we came?"

Cecil chuckled. "Who knows, indeed."

"And what about Hieronymus? We can't give up on him." Anton glanced at Cecil. "I can't, at least."

"I know," said Cecil. "He saved your life, and all. Which I'm very glad about."

"But you didn't really come for him, did you?"

"No, and you didn't come to explore the unknown, like I did," countered Cecil.

"And now we're both having doubts." Anton fell silent, still twitching his tail.

Cecil gazed up at the sky again. "I wonder if old Hieronymus can see these same stars, wherever he is."

"Wherever he is." Anton shuddered in the warm breeze. "You know what we need? We need a new perspective. A fresh pair of eyes. Some good advice."

"Hmmm," said Cecil. "Somebody wise and experienced?"

"Yes," said Anton.

"Okay," said Cecil. "I know just the cat."

"Yep." Anton smiled. "I do too."

❖ ❖ ❖

Cecil woke Katya early and then sat cleaning his fur while Anton explained the whole story. Anton had told her bits and pieces, but now he recounted the entire journey, starting with the call for help over the mouse network. He described Hieronymus, his steadfast and eloquent best mouse friend, who was the object of the rescue effort. Katya shook her head in amazement at that part, but said nothing. She listened to the tales of the ship, the owl and the dog, the trains, the prairie dogs and bison. Cecil told of his encounter with the coyote, but left out most of the details that would have chilled Anton to the bone.

"So," concluded Cecil. "Now we're stuck."

Katya flicked her pointed ears back and forth, thinking. "Tell me again the strange clue that the mice gave you."

"They said that our friend could be found 'between the whale and the coyote.'"

"Well, I know what a coyote is, and you wouldn't want to be between one and anything, I can tell you that. But what is a whale?"

"It's an enormous creature that lives in water, in the ocean," said Cecil, gesturing widely.

Katya shook her head. "Never have seen the ocean."

"Exactly the problem!" said Anton, exasperated. "There's no ocean anywhere near here!"

Cecil ignored Anton and pressed on. "Have you ever seen a fish?" he asked.

"Sure," said Katya. "I've crossed rivers and streams before and I've seen them swimming there. My sister eats them, but they're hard to catch."

"Right. But a whale is not a fish; it's much bigger. Shaped the same, but its head is as big as a train carriage, and its giant flat tail thrashes the water when it dives. Its mouth goes halfway around its head, and it can blow water straight out of a hole on top. That's a whale."

Katya nodded thoughtfully, her gaze moving slowly across the foothills. "Hmmm," she murmured. "A whale, but no ocean. A whale on dry land. Maybe not a real whale, then." She paused and squinted. "Could it look something like *that*?" She raised a paw, pointing over the prairie grass, past the town, down the train tracks. Anton and Cecil sat up tall and stared in that direction, searching for what she was trying to show them. Katya had even better vision than they did, and at first they saw only the misty gray shapes of the higher rocky mountains looming over the rails miles away.

But then the sun rose behind them, its honeyed

light melting the mist, and they saw it. Far away and just beyond the tracks stood a craggy slab of mountaintop, elongated and angled with a thick, rounded base and a wide, curling peak jutting skyward. At this distance it seemed small, but it must have been enormous.

It looked just like a great diving whale.

Anton sat speechless, his mouth hanging open.

Cecil couldn't believe his eyes. He suddenly found himself filled with memories of the fear and loneliness and despair and the deep, thrilling joy of their last adventure on the ocean. He passed a paw over his eyes and took a slow breath. Finally he answered Katya.

"Yeah," he said quietly. "Just like that."

CHAPTER 11

The Sign
of the Coyote

Katya accompanied the brothers back to the train station, advising them along the way that any attempt to get near a coyote might put a severe crimp in their rescue plan. "You two are so little," she said, "you wouldn't stand a chance, especially as coyotes tend to travel in packs."

"Tell me about it," said Cecil, remembering their acrid smell, their rough laughter, the way they'd paced hungrily just outside his prairie dog hole.

"We'll be careful," Anton assured her. "We'll

start by getting close to the whale mountain and see if we can find this witch's house from there."

"I'm not eager to tangle with any animal in this crazy place," Cecil agreed. "I'm going to stay on my own four paws as much as possible."

Katya nodded at this. "A wise cat is a cautious cat," she said. "I don't know much about the 'trains,' but you've come this far already so you probably know what to do. Just be careful, and keep your eyes and ears open."

"I'm almost looking forward to a nice train ride," said Cecil. They had come out of the low hills and the meadow stretched before them, with the squat station building nestled at its edge and a few humans milling about on the platform.

"I'll leave you here," Katya said. "Good luck on your quest."

Anton and Cecil stopped and turned to face Katya, sitting side by side as they often had when leaving their mother for a day on the docks. Sonya would look them over affectionately, patting one on the shoulder or passing her tongue over the forehead of the other.

"We can't thank you enough for helping us," Anton said.

Cecil chimed in. "I was pretty beat up when you came to my rescue."

Katya smiled at them. "Cats have to look out for each other," she said. "Especially the big for the small. There is a Great Cat who lives up in those hills where you're headed. They say he's the wisest and greatest of us all. I've never seen him, but maybe you will. I'm sure he's never met any cats as small as you two."

Cecil felt a shiver in his spine at the thought of meeting such a fabled creature, and he murmured softly, "The Great Cat."

"Good luck to you both," Katya said. She raised her paw and gave Cecil a gentle pat on the shoulder. She turned to Anton, who sat still as her big rough tongue swept across his head between his ears. Then in a flash Katya was bounding away, back to her home in the hills.

Anton and Cecil had no difficulty getting on the train. After the cars were unloaded the men went into the building where the lights were bright and there was food being served. The carriage doors were open and the cats jumped right in. It was easy to hide among the crates and bales still aboard. When the men returned, they barely glanced inside before they slid the big door closed.

"Good night," Cecil said wearily. "I can really use a rest."

"But you're going to be all right, aren't you?" Anton asked.

"Sure, I will. That boy was a kindly one. He gave me a lot to eat. It wasn't tasty—it was kind of like that gluey porridge Cloudy used to serve—but it was filling enough. And they eat this dry stuff—it looks like twigs—I ate some of that, too. You have to chew it a lot, but it's okay. The boy put a wet paste on my leg and wrapped it up. It felt better right away. But then he wrapped the cord around my neck and I panicked. They were folding up their sails and packing up blankets. I thought they were going to take me away with them and you'd never find me."

"But I'd keep looking," Anton assured him. "You know I would."

"I know." Cecil flexed his injured leg a few times, thinking about what it would be like to be a pet. "I've been in lots of tight spots, but . . ." He paused. "That boy had a cord around my neck in the blink of an eye. I couldn't get away. I was more scared than I've ever been in my life."

"Remember when we were stuffed in that cage in the animal market?" Anton asked quietly. "We couldn't get away then either."

"That was different." Cecil tried to think of how. "We were together."

"Together is different," Anton agreed.

"I don't understand it," said Cecil. "I go out on human ships and I swipe their food when I'm hungry. I like how they build huge things that go fast. Humans are powerful. But they're dangerous. More dangerous than I thought."

"How can you be surprised?" asked Anton. "We've been warned about humans impressing us into service on ships since we were little kits, haven't we?"

"Yeah, but . . ." Cecil began, and then fell silent.

Anton gave a soft snort. "You never thought it could happen to you, did you?"

"Not really, no," admitted Cecil.

"It's a strange kind of danger, isn't it?" Anton mused. "The boy fed you plenty and took good care of you. Healed your leg."

"That's true." Cecil pondered a moment. "So I guess the danger is in not being able to leave. We want to go wherever we want, whenever we want."

"To be free." Anton nodded. "All cats are wild, like Katya said. And yet here we are, riding on one of their trains to reach our imprisoned mate."

The shriek of the whistle—once, then again—seemed to agree with Anton's observation. The engine huffed, the steel pistons turned, and with a jolt and a clank the carriages began to roll on the track.

"Here we go," Anton said, wide-eyed. But the two stowaways had not gone very far when they fell to yawning and curled back-to-back against a pile of horse blankets, quickly drifting into sleep.

✤　✤　✤

Anton woke first. He had no idea how long he'd slept, but he could tell the train was slowing down. "Cecil," he whispered to his sleeping brother, who didn't respond. Anton poked him on the head with a paw and repeated, "Cecil, I think we're stopping."

Cecil lifted his head, gazed at the carriage door, and dropped his chin back down on his paws. "I was dreaming," he said. "We were sailing into the harbor and the schooner was full of fish."

"Well, I doubt we'll find any fish here. But maybe we'll find Hieronymus," Anton said. He got to his feet and moved near the door. The wheels were grinding loudly, and the door rattled in its frame. "We're definitely stopping."

Soon the carriage was still and they could hear the men outside, talking and laughing. Anton and Cecil crouched behind a crate. The door slid open and a man stepped inside, glanced about, said something to another man on the platform, and stepped back out again.

"I guess we'd better make a run for it," Cecil said. "Before they come back and start loading stuff in here."

"Right," said Anton. "Just pick a direction and I'll follow you." Cautiously they approached the open door. Cecil peered out while Anton crouched behind him, ready to spring.

"There are some steps toward the front," Cecil said. "Not many humans around. Should be a breeze."

And it was. They dashed across the planks and into a dusty road where a few horses stood about tied up to fence posts. Anton glanced up past the line of rooftops and gasped. The whale-topped mountain was quite close now, looming above the town, its tail arched against the blue sky as if breaching a wide blue sea. *Hieronymus has got to be here somewhere,* Anton thought, beginning to hope. *Now all we need is a coyote.*

Cecil, moving faster than Anton thought he could, darted into an open space under a building without so much as a pause. Anton followed so quickly even the horses didn't notice the two cats. But there was something happening overhead that was the opposite of peaceful. Humans were stamping up and down on the floorboards, men were shouting, and a woman was singing. Anton hunkered down, but Cecil scowled and crept back toward the dusty street. Cecil approached the first horse, who watched him warily from one of his big eyes.

"Don't you get under my hooves now, little cat," said the horse.

Anton stepped out and joined his brother. "You've seen cats like us before?" he asked.

"Sure," said the horse. "I've seen every kind of animal there is. Some humans come out here in those smoke machines, but others just get on their horses and ride, and that's how I got here. I walked across the country from the ocean." He nodded in the direction of the setting sun.

Cecil and Anton looked at each other. Willy had said there was a lot of water at the end of the line.

"There's an ocean in *that* direction?" Anton asked, incredulous.

"Beautiful place," the horse said. "There's a big town, every kind of human and animal you can imagine, and a harbor full of enormous ships with sails. A lot of good grass out that way too, but not in the town."

"You two got names?" asked another horse.

"I'm Anton. This is my brother Cecil."

"I'm Rusty," said the well-traveled horse.

"I'm called Snickers," said the other as he raised his head, craning his neck to look down the street where a cloud of dust appeared to be rolling toward the town. "Whoa, look at that. Here comes a whole lotta trouble."

"You little beasts better run for cover," said Rusty. The cloud was getting close and at the front of it one, two, then more horses' heads broke through, running so fast that the earth trembled beneath their hooves. The door of the saloon flew open, and a few men in big hats came barreling out into the street. One man yanked Rusty's reins from the rail and leaped onto his back, turning him this way and that until he stood up on his hind legs and came down facing the horde of men and horses roaring toward them. There were shouts and confusion and whinnies from the horses.

Anton and Cecil took off down the road, past the line of shops that ended abruptly at a field of dirt and sand. "This way," Cecil said, turning the corner. In a moment they were on a second street, very different from the first, with a couple of trees and a line of buildings that looked more like houses. One had an awning across the front, another had a patch of garden and a gate.

"This is more like it," Anton said. They trotted along quietly, taking in the tamer side of the town. Anton stopped to sniff a spicy herb that reminded him of the paste the villagers had put on Cecil's leg. When he looked up he saw Cecil sitting stock-still, staring wide-eyed at a flat metal sign in the shape of a dog hanging from a gatepost.

"What is it?" Anton asked, walking to Cecil's side.

"That's a coyote."

"Wow," Anton said. "Are you sure?"

"I'm sure."

"You think this is what we're looking for?" Anton gazed at the long snout and big pointed ears of the animal on the rusted sign. "I don't know. It's not a *real* coyote."

"Neither is the whale a real whale, if we're on the right track," said Cecil. He moved a dozen paces into the dirt road, then turned and faced the sign. "Come see this."

Anton followed and stood next to Cecil. He looked past the sign and saw a little walkway ending at a two-story house with an awning across the front. Rising behind the house was the whale-like gray face of the mountain, with the twin points of the tail pointing up at the blue sky overhead.

"Between the whale and the coyote," Anton said slowly, his eyes moving from the mountain to the sign to the house in between.

"This is it," Cecil agreed. "Hieronymus is in that house."

⚜ ⚜ ⚜

The sign squeaked on its hinges in the dusty breeze, and the coyote pictured on it seemed to be gazing down, smiling mischievously at the brother cats. Or hungrily, perhaps. Either way, it gave Anton the shivers as he stepped onto the porch with Cecil. Unfamiliar sounds floated across from the main street of the town—heavy boots thunking in time with jingling bells, the squeaks of swinging doors, horses clopping at a full gallop down the road, strange music that was more like the clamor of shorebirds than the sailors' tuneful songs from back home. The cats pressed close to the rough planked wall under a window and craned their necks up and around, inspecting the house.

"What now?" asked Anton. "We'll have to find a way in somehow."

"Yup, that about sums it up," said Cecil. He stood on his hind legs and peered in the low window, which was shut, his nose working along the sill. "Hmmm, smells good in there."

"*You* think it smells good everywhere," said Anton.

Cecil dropped down and shook his head. "Not over by those horses I didn't. Phew, that was awful."

A shriek cut through the warm air, high and fluted like a train whistle, and Anton turned to look down the street. But the train had left the station; there was nothing on the tracks. And besides, the sound seemed to have come from over their heads, inside the house. How could that be?

They heard footsteps approaching from within.

"Get ready," murmured Cecil, prodding Anton toward the door.

The door opened and closed quickly, and a little girl stepped onto the porch. She wore a long, many-layered dress and her blond hair was gathered with a silky blue ribbon. She walked over to a rocking chair and sat down, arranging the folds of her dress carefully, and began speaking in a pleasant voice. The cats watched her curiously.

"Who's she talking to?" whispered Cecil. "There's nobody else over there."

"Not to us, I hope," said Anton.

"No, she's looking down." Cecil lifted his head to see better. "There's something in her lap."

The girl held up the thing in her lap, and the cats saw a tiny version of the girl in her hands, complete with a miniature flouncy dress and ribboned hair.

"What shall we do today, dolly?" said the girl to the thing, stroking its yellow hair. "Shall we play with Merlin and Snowball?"

Anton nudged Cecil's shoulder. "What's she holding? I can't tell. A baby human?"

Cecil squinted. "I don't think so. I've seen those, and they wriggle. This is just one of those unmoving ones they play with." He stood and stretched his back. "The human seems safe enough. I'm going to go make friends."

"That's not what we're here to do!" whispered Anton as his brother sauntered across the porch.

Cecil approached the girl slowly with soft eyes, tail up. The girl saw him and squealed, tossing the doll down behind her and plopping to her knees in front of Cecil, her fingers extended.

"Kitty!" she said with delight. "Hello, what's your name?"

Cecil rubbed the side of his face along her hand and pressed against her legs as she rubbed his ears.

"Ooh, kitty," crooned the girl. "You are a dirty one. Would you like a bath?"

Cecil was obviously enjoying the rubbing. He glanced over at Anton and sent him a satisfied smile. Anton scowled but said nothing.

"I like you, fluffy kitty," the girl continued. "I think I'll keep you." And she slid her hands under his belly, lifted him up, and tucked him under one arm. "Ooo, goodness! And I'll put you on a diet, too."

Cecil yowled and squirmed mightily in her arms. His hind claws snagged in the layers of her skirts and quickly tore a hole in the fabric. The girl shrieked and flung Cecil down.

"You beast!" she cried, stamping one slippered foot. "You ripped my favorite dress!"

Cecil dashed off the porch and around the corner of the house, where Anton had already scampered.

"Well, so much for making *friends*," said Anton as they trotted briskly into the tall grass behind the house.

"Hmph," said Cecil. "I didn't care for her anyway. That squeaky voice would drive me crazy."

"Yeah, I'll bet," said Anton, smirking. "Plus those horrible rubbing fingers. Who could stand it?"

Cecil chuckled. "Anyway, I did manage to learn one piece of good news from those rubbing fingers."

Anton looked at Cecil. "What's that?"

"He's in there," Cecil said. "I know the scent of that blasted rodent, and he's in there. Alive."

❖ ❖ ❖

The brothers sat in a narrow alley between two buildings across the street, where they'd moved to survey the coyote house.

"Did you really think he might *not* be alive?" asked Anton.

Cecil shrugged. "I thought it was possible." He looked sidelong at Anton. "Come on. You were worried too, weren't you?"

Anton had to admit that he was, terribly, and that even the worrying had worried him. "We've got to get in there right now," he said fiercely.

"I agree," said Cecil. "I'm starving, and they probably have food."

Anton sighed. "So what's our plan?"

Cecil rubbed a paw over his face and smoothed his whiskers. "Okay. Unless we get lucky, we probably can't use the door. And the windows on the bottom are closed, so that's no good."

Anton nodded, and his gaze moved to the upper floor of the house. There were windows up there, and he could see curtains moving in one of them, blown by the wind.

"What about up top?" he asked.

"Yep, that's our way in," Cecil said. "Now, how to get to it?" He tracked backward from the house to its neighbors along the street, and finally to a tall, sprawling tree in the yard next to the third house down, and pointed a paw. "There's the answer. We climb that tree, jump from house to house on the rooftops, and drop down to the window on that ledge with the railing in front of it. Easy!" Cecil beamed.

"Easy?" snorted Anton. "We'll break our necks!"

"Come on, we're cats! It's what we *do*."

"It's too risky."

Cecil swished his tail impatiently. "You want to get in? This is the way we do it."

Anton looked at the coyote-signed house once more, took a big breath and let it out in a long, worried gust. "Of course I want to get in. I do. But what if . . ." A fear greater than the rooftops had lodged in his brain. "What if we can't get out again? What if we become prisoners, too?"

Cecil met his eyes and nodded. "I know. We'll be careful. We'll stick together, like brother cats." He stretched his back legs and started walking. "But he's in there, Anton, and he's waiting for us. You coming or not?"

Anton swallowed hard. They'd come so far. Hieronymus was probably in a house not fifty feet away. The mouse had called for help, and help had arrived. Anton got to his feet. "I'm coming."

CHAPTER 12

Caged and Free

Climbing the tree wasn't the hard part. The cats had sharp claws and strong legs, and the boughs of the tree reached out over the roof of the first house so they could drop onto it without too much trouble. Walking on the steep metal roof was tricky—they had to creep slowly and use the pads of their paws for traction.

The real challenge was the jumping.

"Okay," said Cecil, gulping. "Here I go." From the edge of the first roof, the distance to the second looked much farther than it had from the ground. And the ground was very far down.

Anton didn't reply. He was crouched, peering over the edge and trembling. Cecil fixed his eyes on the second roof. It was made of small overlapping wooden tiles, uneven but not as steep as the first. Cecil backed away from the edge and began a running start, but as he jumped he felt a stab of pain in his injured leg and he careened into the air, his arc too flat, stretching desperately and catching the second roof with only his front claws.

"Cecil!" cried Anton. "Hang on!"

Cecil's back legs flailed until he gripped the planked wall underneath, then he hauled himself up paw over paw to the rooftop, dislodging a few tiles as he went. He leaped to his feet and turned to Anton, smiling in spite of his leg. "Not bad, eh?" he called across. "Come on, you'll be fine."

Anton set his back feet carefully against a rusted spot in the metal, coiled his muscles, and sprang across the gap in an artful, cat-like bound.

"Wow! Nicely done." Cecil pounced on Anton's tail to keep him from tumbling off the roof after his not-so-artful landing, and they got to their feet again. Clambering quickly across the rough wooden tiles, they reached the edge and were checking the distance to the third roof—the coyote house roof—when the door on the porch swung open below them. They stepped back and flattened down, peeking over the edge to see who was coming out.

It was the girl again, wearing a different dress and clutching the doll in one arm, a man and woman on either side of her. The man shut the door with a boom behind them, and the three people strolled out to the street and down the block out of sight, the girl yammering all the while in a whining, unhappy tone.

"That's good, at least," said Anton. "The fewer humans the better."

"Agreed," said Cecil. "So, about this next jump."

"Yes?" Anton put his paws close to the edge and looked across. "That roof is much flatter than this one, right?"

"Right, but you see how it's also *lower* than this one?"

Anton nodded. "So, easier to jump down to."

"True." Cecil glanced at Anton. "But also impossible to jump *up from*. So once we jump, we can't get back this way. We either have to get in through the window or . . ." They both looked at the ground again.

"Got it," said Anton grimly. "I'll go first this time."

He coiled again and bounded onto the third roof, managing to stay on his feet. Cecil landed next to him with a thud, and they both moved to the front edge facing the street. They positioned themselves above the open window, crouched low, and pricked up their ears to listen.

What they heard surprised them very much.

First came the sound of a bell, clear and loud, reverberating out through the window. Anton and Cecil looked at each other. Then came the clip-clop of a horse trotting by, again from inside the house. Next they heard a man's voice.

Nothing but cattle rustlers and horse thieves, I tell you, drawled the voice, though the words meant nothing to the listening felines. *Call in the cavalry!*

Cecil's heart jumped. It was clearly a human talking, which would complicate the rescue effort.

Another voice sang out, high-pitched like a lady's. *It'll be a hoedown. A shindig. A grand old time!*

Cecil shook his head. "There must be a whole crowd in there," he whispered.

Anton nodded miserably. "I'll take a look."

Very carefully, Anton leaned over the edge of

the roof and peered, upside down, into the window. He hung there for a moment, then pulled up quickly, his eyes narrowed in confusion.

"I saw him!" said Anton. "I saw Hieronymus. He's alive! He's in a cage on a table. But . . ." He paused.

"But what?" Cecil asked, impatient.

"But the only other creature in the room is a bird."

"A bird?" repeated Cecil. "What kind of bird?"

"A big gray one, hooked beak and talons, the usual. It's perched on top of a hanging cage. But I couldn't see any humans at all."

"That's impossible," whispered Cecil. "Who's doing the talking?"

At that moment they heard a familiar voice, one they could understand. "Truly outstanding work, Dayo, but would you be so kind as to give it a rest for a while? Your racket is giving me a headache." It was Hieronymus.

Anton's eyes lit up. "That's him! He must be talking to the bird."

"My friend," replied a hollow, squawking voice that the cats understood as well, "it's not 'racket.' You know Miss Betsy loves my speaking, and I have to practice. Why don't you get some exercise? You're getting chubby." Then came the unintelligible human voice again: *Back in the saddle, boys! Round 'em up and move 'em out!* They heard Hieronymus groan, and then a soft whirring sound.

Cecil leaned over slowly and carefully, as Anton had done, until he could see into the lower part of the room. Hieronymus was indeed trapped in a large white cage with thin, close-set bars. A tiny bowl of water and another filled with small pellets sat on the floor of the cage, which was scattered with strips of newspaper. The whirring sound came from the only thing moving in the cage—a small freestanding wheel, suspended upright, which spun wildly as the mouse himself ran and ran along its inside track.

Cecil leaned a little farther, looking for the bird. It was large, though not as big as the owl in the first train station, and well-groomed, with gray, scalloped feathers layered from its rounded head down to its elegant tail, where a single stripe of red feathers flared stylishly. Its eyes were perfectly round, black in the center with white rims, and sat on either side of a large black beak. It cocked

its head as it gazed down at Hieronymus from its
cage-top perch, and then it opened its mouth and
emitted an exact duplicate of the whirring sound.

Cecil whispered to Anton, "It's the bird. The
bird makes the sounds."

Anton brought his head down next to Cecil's
so they hung side by side, peering in. The bird
lifted one taloned foot into the air theatrically and
recited, *Never squat with your spurs on, son.*

"I've never seen a bird do that before," said
Anton.

"The bird could stand on its head and ride a
horse, for all I care," muttered Cecil. "Those talons
and that beak are what worry me."

Before Anton could respond, an earsplitting
scream filled the room. The bird had spotted the
cats.

"Oh, my beak and tail feathers!" the bird
screeched. "Hieronymus, run!"

The mouse stopped cold on his wheel. "I *was*
running, Dayo. What's wrong?"

"Lions! Two lion cubs at the window!"

Hieronymus leaped from the wheel and spun
to the window in terror. He squinted at the two

suspended heads and stood still, his tiny forepaws slack at his sides. Then he came alive again and hurried to the edge of the cage and gripped the bars.

"At last!" he cried out, weeping and laughing at the same time. "You found me!"

The cats dropped down to the ledge and climbed onto the sill. "We found you!" whooped Anton as he and Cecil squeezed through the opening and landed on the floor below.

Dayo flapped his wings in agitation, causing the hanging cage to jounce and swing from side to side, which made the bird flap even more. "*Off my land, cowboy!*" he shrieked incoherently.

"Uh oh," said Cecil, looking up.

Dayo flung himself off the perch and dive-bombed the cats. Gray feathers poofed in all directions as he dropped through the air, swiping Cecil with his wings as he passed. He pulled up sharply and landed in a muddle on a bookshelf. Anton and Cecil darted under a low sofa and peeked out warily.

"Sheesh, nice to meet you, too!" called Cecil, shaking his head. He looked at Anton. "What is it with birds, anyway? Why all the craziness?"

"Dayo!" cried Hieronymus from his cage, as loudly as he could muster. "Stop that right now! These are not lions. They are my friends!"

The bird righted himself and swooped to the back of the sofa where Anton and Cecil were hiding.

"They belong to the *cat* family—anyone can see that!" said Dayo, pacing across the sofa, his talons plucking at the fabric. "And a *cat* is friend to neither bird nor mouse."

"You got the *bird* part right, anyway," grumbled Cecil. Anton shushed him.

"CATS, get out immediately!" ordered Dayo shrilly, and turned to the mouse. "I'm protecting you, Hieronymus. You can thank me later." He nervously plucked a few of his feathers and flung them into the air.

"I shall not thank you at all, Dayo," Hieronymus huffed. "These are my cat friends and I trust them completely. They have come a very long way to rescue me from *this*." And he gestured at the cage around him.

Dayo clucked and paced. "They'll eat you, you silly mouse. I know they will. They'll eat me too if I let my guard down."

Cecil surveyed the room and called to Hieronymus dryly. "Say, old pal, didn't we hear on the mouse network that you were being held in a dungeon by an evil witch and guarded by a dragon? Kind of an exaggeration, wasn't it?"

"A *dragon*?" squawked Dayo, insulted.

Hieronymus blinked. "Oh, dear me. That's not the message I sent."

"You sent a *message*?" screeched the bird.

"All right, everybody calm down, please," said Anton, his voice muffled by the sofa. "So, Dayo, let's get properly introduced. You are a . . . what?"

Dayo's eyes narrowed and he cocked his head. "Is this some sort of cat trick?"

"No trick," said Anton. "I really want to know."

Dayo hesitated, chewing one claw. "I'm a parrot. An African gray parrot, if you must know."

"Ah, and handsome you are, in your . . . grayness," said Anton. Cecil rolled his eyes. "And you have a talent for making noises, is that right?" Anton asked.

The parrot stretched his ruffled neck and preened his feathers with his beak. "Why, yes. I can imitate many sounds. I do have a talent for it."

Hieronymus caught Anton's eye and nodded in understanding. "Show them your speaking, Dayo," he encouraged the parrot.

Dayo produced a pleased rolling trill and flew across to the table next to Hieronymus's cage. He eyed the cats distrustfully, then cleared his throat and opened his beak. *Round up the posse, boys!* he spoke in a deep, rough voice.

Anton poked his head out, his mouth hanging open. "But that's human language!"

"It is," said Dayo, strutting up and down.

"What does it mean?" asked Cecil.

"I've no idea. All I know is that every time I speak for them, I get a cracker."

Cecil looked at Hieronymus in surprise. "Is that true?"

Hieronymus sighed and nodded. "Every single time."

"Wow," said Cecil grudgingly. "Neat trick."

"We've never met a creature who could speak human before," said Anton, creeping out from under the sofa. "Impressive."

"Why, thank you," said Dayo, bowing slightly. "It is really a gift."

"Will you speak some more for us?" Anton slipped across the floor, moving smoothly toward the table.

Hieronymus kept one eye on Anton and chimed in. "Yes, a little more, please," he said, gesturing furtively to Cecil to come out as well.

Cecil could see that Anton was headed for the cage and that Dayo was still a dangerous obstacle. They needed a distraction. He paced along the floor, his eyes fixed on the parrot, waiting for an opportunity.

"Oh, well, I . . ." began Dayo.

A door slammed downstairs and the creatures froze. There was a beat of silence.

The cats whipped into action. Cecil vaulted straight up to the table in front of Dayo, driving the parrot into the air and back up to its perch, where it clung to its cage in shock. Anton leaped to the table as well and began searching Hieronymus's cage for a door.

"Here, Anton, it's over here," called Hieronymus. "But I don't know how it works! I've tried gnawing it, believe me, but it does no good."

Cecil could hear the family walking downstairs.

The little girl would probably come up to check on her pets. Anton would need to work quickly.

"There's a latch, do you see?" said Hieronymus, hopping from one foot to the other and wringing his tail. Anton hooked his claws around the wire bars and pulled, but the door held fast. He jabbed at the latch with his paw.

Dayo watched the cage, angling his head this way and that and muttering. "This is outrageous. You can't just take Hieronymus." He plucked more feathers. "I can't let you take him. I should sound the alarm. Of course! That's my job, that's what I'll do." And he cleared his throat.

The cats exchanged a glance, and Cecil whirled to Dayo.

"Hey, bird," he called quickly, racking his brain. "Listen. Why don't you . . . come with us, instead? Fly in the sky, be free."

Dayo stared down at Cecil. "Be free?" He cocked his head and jutted his beak forward.

Cecil nodded, smiling. "Wouldn't that be great? Just let us get out of here, and we'll help you get out too." He flicked his tail toward Hieronymus. "Do it for your friend, here."

"But," Dayo said, bobbing his head anxiously, "Miss Betsy would want us to stay."

"Dayo, please." Hieronymus spoke softly from his cage. "You have to understand. I really want to go."

The parrot blinked at the mouse, his beak open. "You do?" he squawked softly.

Hieronymus nodded and opened his paws. "I can't live like this, and I need your help."

Footsteps sounded on the stairs, coming closer.

Cecil looked over his shoulder at Anton, his head spinning with exhilaration. "Come on, come on! Now or never, little kit."

"Hush, Cecil!" spat Anton, sheer panic in his voice. His paw shook as he pressed and pressed on the latch. Suddenly a horizontal bar moved slightly. Anton gasped. "It's just like the latch on Willy's crate on the train!" He jammed down hard with both paws, the other end of the bar lifted out of its slot, and just like that the cage door swung open.

"Yes!" cried Hieronymus, dashing out and clutching Anton's foreleg. "Oh, so good to breathe free air again!"

"You know, it's the same . . ." Cecil began, when the door to the room opened wide.

There stood Miss Betsy, gaping at the scene. No one moved for a long moment.

Dayo broke the silence. *Well howdy, little lady!* he drawled.

"Merlin!" screeched the girl, looking at Dayo. She frowned at the parrot as if he'd been derelict in his duties. Dayo looked away. *Pretty bird,* he muttered.

She swung her gaze to Hieronymus and gasped. "Snowball!" she howled. "You're out of your cage!"

All hat and no cattle, droned Dayo quietly.

"And YOU!" The girl stabbed a thin finger accusingly at Cecil. "You filthy beast, how did you get in here? Get out of my way!" She lunged forward, grabbing for Hieronymus.

Cecil drew back in surprise, then fluffed out his tail savagely. "Oh no you don't!" he growled. He took a deep breath and snarled, loud and long from his chest, just the way Katya had done for him in the village. And it had the same effect—the girl screamed and stumbled backward.

"Quick!" shouted Cecil. "Everybody move!"

In a flash both cats sprang from the table, darted past the little girl, and slipped through the doorway. Hieronymus scrambled down the table leg and streaked across the floor, not far behind them. Dayo lifted off from his perch and flew in tight circles around the room, squawking incoherently, then whooshed out the door as well.

"Merlin!" wailed the girl. "Snowball! Wait!"

The man and woman were hurrying up the stairs when the creatures came zipping down, underfoot and overhead. The woman screamed and jumped aside, but the man turned in pursuit. The front door was shut tight, and the cats skidded to a stop and looked around frantically for another way out. They ran toward the back of the house, through a small room with a fireplace and several high tables, and into a long room furnished with many chairs of various sizes. At the far end of the room Cecil saw a curtain move—an open window.

"Up there!" he yelled. "Hurry!"

The cats bounded over two low chairs and scrabbled across a table covered in cloth and strewn with small, shiny items. They heard things tumbling away and breaking on the floor as they snagged the cloth with their claws and dragged it with them along the table, but finally they were at the window. Cecil pulled up short and looked over his shoulder just as Anton sprang through and disappeared.

Hieronymus was running hard, making the turn into the room as fast as his legs could carry him. His face was set, but Cecil saw that the little rodent was not as quick as he used to be, and the man was close behind, almost upon Hieronymus. As he drew close to the mouse, the man pulled his hat from his head and stretched it in front of him, ready to trap the pesky pet with it. Cecil cried out, but he was too far away to do any good.

At that moment Dayo banked into the room, narrowly avoiding the furniture and flapping his wings furiously to stay aloft. He saw Hieronymus and the outstretched hat, and he dove. Just as the man leaped forward to clap the hat over the mouse once and for all, Dayo swooped in, snagged Hieronymus's tail with his beak, and flew straight up over the chairs to the window. Hieronymus yelped as his head bumped across the sill, and then they were through.

The girl rushed into the room, shrieking. Her head swiveled from the man sprawled on the floor to the open window. Cecil glimpsed her stamping her little foot before he turned and bounded out after his friends.

❖ ❖ ❖

The pale orange sun slipped behind the whale-shaped mountaintop as the group gathered among the boulders in the hills behind the house, first catching their breath, then laughing in astonishment. Cecil was shocked that the "plan," such as it was, had actually worked.

"I couldn't believe it when I felt Dayo's beak clamp down and I was plucked into the air," said Hieronymus, wiping tears of relief from his cheeks and rubbing his sore tail with his paws. "I didn't know you could fly that well," he said to the parrot.

"Nor did I," admitted Dayo, arranging and smoothing his feathers. He turned to Cecil. "That snarl of yours was impressive."

Cecil chuckled. "And effective. A lynx taught me that." He looked sheepishly at Anton. "I guess we should have checked *all* the windows before we tried the roof, huh?"

Anton shook his head, smiling. "I'll never forget the girl's face when she opened the door and saw us all," he said. "She turned so red!"

"Little Miss Betsy," said Dayo, clucking his beak softly.

"Sheesh," said Cecil, shuddering. "What a screamer."

"She does have a strong voice," Dayo agreed.

"Only if you like screeching," said Anton, his face turning serious. "And she kept poor Hieronymus locked up like a prisoner. What a tyrant."

"Even so, she did seem to delight in our company," Dayo pointed out.

"Dayo?" said Hieronymus, scrutinizing the bird. "What are you thinking? Aren't you glad to be free?"

"Yes. Flying outside is fun." He shifted on his skinny legs. "But it's getting late. I'd better be heading back."

"What do you mean?" cried Hieronymus. "You're not going back there, are you?"

Dayo bobbed his head thoughtfully and raised his eyes to the dusky evening sky. "I am. She's not that bad, you know. She appreciates my talents."

"Well, so would others," said Hieronymus gently. "You could travel with us for a while, see the world. You don't have to stay a prisoner."

The parrot smiled and idly dragged his talons along the rock face. "I was never a prisoner—the window was always open, remember? And I *have* seen the world, and it's dangerous. When I was taken from my homeland, I traveled here in a box on a great ship over an endless ocean. I didn't think I would survive. And the trip took so long, I don't think I could ever go back, even if I knew the way. Besides, there are no other parrots out here, no family for me. With Miss Betsy, I have a home, I'm not afraid, and I have someone to talk to. And Hieronymus, you know, I really like to talk." He gazed at the mouse and gave a short bow. "It was an honor sharing a room with you. You're a gentlemouse, and I learned quite a lot from you."

"Likewise," said Hieronymus, his voice quavering.

Cecil exchanged a glance with Anton, and knew his brother was thinking the same thing. Animals made choices—a "bargain with humans" as Katya would say—and you had to make the choice you could live with.

Dayo turned to Anton and Cecil. "There are very large cats where I come from, lions and cheetahs—frightening brutes, fearless and loyal. You two are every bit as brave as they are. It's been a pleasure." He cocked his head at Cecil.

"And you turned out to be better than the average bird," said Cecil, grinning.

The door on the house slammed in the distance, and they heard the little girl's high voice calling.

"Merlin! Merlin, where are you? Come back!" A pause, and a small sob. "Please come back!"

"Off I go," said Dayo. "Best of luck to you all." He flapped into the dusk, blending in with the pale gray sky, and disappeared. One final call drifted back to them on the breeze. *That train has left the station, boys.*

Cecil took a breath and looked at the others. "Ready?"

Hieronymus nodded. "Let's get far away from here." He turned and scampered off, the cats right behind him.

CHAPTER 13

The Great Cat

ieronymus ran ahead of his rescuers without looking back or pausing for breath. When they were beyond the town, Anton shouted, "You can stop now. No one is following us." The mouse slowed, glancing over his shoulder, and then stopped abruptly, sitting up on his hind legs as the cats caught up with him.

"I can't tell you how wonderful it feels to run on solid earth," Hieronymus said. "There's something humiliating about running in a wheel. It feels so pointless."

"It didn't look too dignified," Anton agreed.

Cecil chortled. "I'd have to be pretty desperate before I'd run in something like that."

"Well," said Hieronymus. "I was desperate. I'd been in that cage a month before I even got a message out to the network. They sent in a team who tried to get the cage door open one night while Dayo was asleep, but even a mouse can't chew through steel, and we couldn't figure out the latch."

"Sometimes," said Cecil, "you just need a cat."

"You can say that again," said Hieronymus.

"Sometimes you just need a cat," Cecil repeated.

"I've never been so happy to see a cat in my life as I was when I saw your faces upside down in that window."

"Well, you're a free mouse now," said Anton, brimming with happiness at the sight of his friend sitting close by. "But what I'm wondering is how you wound up in a cage."

"It's a long story," said the mouse, rubbing his paws together as if to warm himself up for the tale.

"Maybe we could find a bite to eat before you start," said Cecil.

"I'm pretty thirsty myself," said Anton. They looked about. They were sitting in a narrow, sandy field halfway between the back of the town and the rising foothills of the mountain shaped like a whale. The sun was low in the sky and the mountain cast a long, cool shadow across the plain. Without consulting, all three turned away from the town and walked toward the mountain. There were some scrubby bushes huddled together at the base, which they knew might mean water nearby. Anton and Cecil strode side by side; it was too hot for them to run, but Hieronymus streaked ahead. He disappeared briefly under one of the bushes. As the brothers closed in, he came out looking pleased.

"There's a little stream," he announced, "and some nice black berries."

"Berries," Cecil said. "I don't like the sound of that." But in fact when they arrived at the tall brambles climbing the face of a rock, the berries proved to be delicious. Anton ate a few, while Cecil investigated the sparkling stream that ran downhill and pooled in a depression between two flat stones. "Will you look at this," he called back joyfully. "Minnows!"

"I'll stick with the berries, thanks," said Hieronymus. He was sitting on the ground with a berry as big as his head between his paws.

"I haven't had fresh fish since I don't know when," said Anton, and in a few leaps he joined his brother who was scooping little black minnows into his mouth with his paw.

"I'm not sure minnows qualify as fish," Cecil said, moving aside to give his brother room. "But they sure taste great to me."

Hieronymus, his face smeared with purple juice, scurried to the water's edge and took a long drink. "This seems like a pretty good place. A mouse could live here quite comfortably."

"It might get lonely," Cecil said. The sun had dropped behind the mountain and dusk had descended with unnerving speed. An owl hooted somewhere above them.

"It's a little creepy too," observed Anton.

Then all three jumped straight up in place as an agonized scream tore through the air. It was deep, sonorous, furious—a cry of frustration and rage.

"My whiskers," whispered Hieronymus, who was the first to return to the ground. "That's one big, angry creature."

"It's a cat," said Anton.

Cecil nodded in agreement. "It's a very large cat."

Again the cry filled the air, and this time the brothers tracked it with their ears, their heads turning together toward a break in the boulders just above the pool.

"It's up there," Cecil said. "And it's in trouble."

"We'd better go see what we can do," Cecil said, his eyes bright at the thought of another rescue mission.

"Dayo told me all the cats are really big around here," Hieronymus said softly. "Maybe I'll just wait for you here."

Anton studied his anxious friend. "Don't you know by now that if you're with us, no cat is going to harm you? If we leave you behind, you're defenseless. Also, you might be helpful."

Hieronymus shuddered. "I've been in that cage so long, I've lost my courage."

Cecil was already moving in the direction of the roar. He looked back at his brother and the mouse. "Oh, come on," he said. "What would your ancestors say?"

This reminder of Hieronymus's glorious family tree, tales of which he had told Anton on their first shipboard meeting, affected Hieronymus like a tonic. He passed his paws over his whiskers and ears, rotated his shoulders to limber up, and bounded behind Cecil, who was carefully making his way over the boulders that blocked the way. Anton brought up the rear, snuffling up the berries Hieronymus hadn't finished.

The rescue party heard the scream again. The voice sounded vexed past endurance, and they corrected their course. "We're close," Cecil said.

"Stay low," Anton called to him. "We don't know what we're going to find."

Hieronymus was emboldened by his ability to blend in with the scenery. "I'm the same color as these rocks," he observed. "Can you see me? I'll bet you can't even see me." He darted ahead, passing Cecil, who was pulling himself up a jagged rock face. At the top he stopped and let out a soft squeak of alarm.

"What is it?" Cecil asked, climbing up behind the mouse. Then he, too, let out a mew of surprise. He looked back at Anton, who was head and shoulders above the top, pushing up with his hind legs braced against a convenient outcrop. "Wait till you see this!" he said softly. Anton quickly and quietly joined his comrades and looked down upon the astonishing scene.

Below them in a narrow clearing an enormous cat, the largest they had ever seen, struggled helplessly. He was tawny gold from ears to tail, except for his muzzle, which was white. He had a long tail, thick as a ship's mooring rope, and paws the size of lobsters. When he turned his great head, Anton caught a glimpse of his eyes, golden and black-rimmed, glinting in the dying sunlight.

"Cats have mercy!" Anton exclaimed. "That must be the Great Cat."

"Whatever he is, he's certainly in a Great Fix," observed Hieronymus.

The huge cat's back leg was caught in a knot of rope attached to a tall pine and he was clearly unable to free himself from it. He was standing on three legs, pulling forward until the captured leg was parallel to the ground, then he turned back and fell to tearing at the rope with his front claws. But his efforts only served to tighten the knot. In frustration he fell down upon his side and let out a deep whine. Exhausted, he dropped his head to the ground with a thud and closed his eyes.

Cecil was already halfway down the rocky descent and Hieronymus scampered after him. Anton paused, taking in the powerful animal—bigger than a human and much stronger—and he reflected that being large and fierce wasn't always the easiest way to live in the world. Then he hurried down and joined his friends, who stood together at the Great Cat's head. The trapped animal gazed at them in silence, blinking his golden eyes as if he couldn't believe what he saw. When he spoke his voice was deep and warm and thrilling.

"Where on earth did you come from?" he said.

Cecil appeared awestruck, opening and closing his mouth a few times before finally murmuring, "Well, that's a long story."

"I've never seen such tiny cats," he said. "I must be dreaming."

Anton stepped closer. "No, we're real enough. We'll try to help you get free."

"I don't see how you can help," the Great Cat said. "I've been caught here since this morning. The more I struggle, the worse it gets. This cord is strong. If I can't tear it off, how could you?"

"Ahem," said a high, squeaky voice. Three sets of cats' eyes swiveled to focus on the little gray creature, who was examining a bit of the cord at a safe distance from the Great Cat's head. "I'm your mouse," Hieronymus said, standing up to his full height. "This job is a cinch. I will have to ask you to be patient and maintain a calm and pleasant demeanor."

"Do you have any idea who you're talking to?" said the Great Cat, pulling himself up on his front paws. "I've a good mind to make a snack of you."

Anton gulped. "No, don't eat him," he said quickly. "If Hieronymus says he can do it, he can do it. He can gnaw through anything."

The Great Cat closed his eyes and sighed through his nose. "It's not as if I have any choice," he said. "He's welcome to try."

Hieronymus set to work, examining the Great Cat's hind leg, where the rope knot was so tight it had bitten cruelly into the thin flesh. The cord was taut, rising a little as it neared the tree. Hieronymus moved a few steps back and chose a spot where it passed close to the ground. He was able to sit up and grasp the thin, twisty rope between his paws. "It's made of horse-tail hair," he observed. "Very oily and strong."

Anton, who had been thinking there was a strong smell of horse in the air, said, "That explains it."

"What an officious creature that mouse is," said the Great Cat.

"He comes from a long line of know-it-alls," Cecil assured him.

Then, as Hieronymus began to chew the rope, Anton and Cecil exchanged names with the Great Cat, who was called Montana.

"I am, I believe, the biggest cat in the world," declared Montana. Anton nodded vigorously—this must be true.

"All animals fear me," Montana continued, "and all humans, too."

"And yet," Hieronymus squeaked, spitting out bits of rope from between his teeth, "here you are in a trap, set by humans." He glanced at the others, his eyes twinkling. "Happens to the best of us, I expect."

Montana scowled at Hieronymus, who went back to work on the rope. "A mistake, yes. One I won't make again. I have no interest in their world. I prefer to be alone."

Anton wondered if this was really true or if it was simply what the Great Cat had grown accustomed to, but said nothing.

Montana described how one night he had climbed the tallest mountain and stood at the top from where he could see a great distance, and he knew that he was the most powerful creature in his domain. He did not like to be seen. His loyalty, he said, was to the sky, as only the sky was beyond his control.

"And now," Montana concluded, "it appears that I'm going to be indebted to two tiny cats and a silly mouse." He chuckled, a sound so rich and full of vibration that Cecil and Anton, without warning, began to purr.

As Hieronymus gnawed, he thought of the long history of his family and of his own adventures in the world, of his recent captivity and now this rescue of the largest cat in the world. Pride swelled his heart. He chewed through the last stubborn strands of the rope and held the two ends apart over his head. "The Great Cat is free!" he proclaimed.

Montana jerked his back leg forward and swished his heavy tail, accidentally sending Hieronymus sprawling face down on the ground. In a great bound Montana crossed the clearing. He leaped joyfully from boulder to boulder while Anton and Cecil watched, purring.

Hieronymus pulled himself to his feet, then dusted himself off with his paws. "Well. Can you beat that?"

Montana sprang high up, disappearing and re-appearing above them. The night was quiet and still. Suddenly the three friends heard a sharp, yipping sound, far off at first and then closer.

Cecil shivered. "Coyotes," he said grimly.

"Is he just going to leave us here after we saved his life?" Hieronymus asked. Then they saw the Great Cat, high up, looking down at them from a steep cliff, his yellow eyes gleaming in the dark.

"He did say he prefers to be alone," Anton observed.

As they watched, Montana disappeared again, but they could hear him crashing through the rough stones and spindly trees. He entered the clearing in a great leap and sat down before them, looking eminently pleased with himself. "I've reached a decision," he said.

"We'd like to hear it," Hieronymus said coolly.

"I've never shared my den with another animal in this world, but it's not safe for you three out here tonight, and as I am indebted to you, I invite you to come with me now."

Anton breathed a long sigh of contentment.

"We accept," Cecil said.

And so the two cats and the mouse set out

behind their protector, who slowed his pace so that they could keep up. After a long, twisting, rocky climb they came to a narrow opening in the face of the mountain. "This is it," Montana said, stepping aside so that they might enter.

Anton and Cecil went in, but Hieronymus paused at the entrance, looking back the way they had come, and then up at the sky, where the moon was milky white and the stars twinkled brightly.

"You can really see the heavens from up here," Hieronymus observed. "The stars tell many a story."

Montana made a snuffling sound, which might have been a laugh. "They do," he agreed. "That group just overhead, that's the Great Lion. He climbed a mountain so high he stepped into the sky."

"Really?" said Hieronymus. "We call that the Sagacious Mouse. He is so wise he gives off light. The old name for him is Mus Sapiens."

"Hmmm," said Montana. "I've not heard that story. In fact, I've never talked to a mouse before."

Hieronymus huffed. "I'm sure they mostly just run screaming when they see you."

"That's true," he said. "And I don't blame them

for that. However, you are a brave mouse and a clever one. I welcome you to my den."

Again Hieronymus felt a thrill of accomplishment. How many mice in the world could say they'd spent the night in the den of the Great Cat and lived to tell the tale? It was a story worth repeating.

Montana's secret lair was a wide, high, cool space, with a rounded ceiling and a smooth floor. Anton and Cecil had settled side by side on a slab that jutted out from one corner. Montana threw himself down toward the back and Hieronymus curled up near the entrance.

"Now," he said. "Shall I tell you how I wound up in that cage?"

Cecil and Anton settled themselves in for the story, tucking in their paws and arranging their tails comfortably. To everyone's surprise, Montana lifted his head and said, "A cage? Yes. I'd like to hear about that."

CHAPTER 14

Another Sea

I t all began," Hieronymus said, settling himself on his haunches and clearing his throat for a long recitation, "when I was contacted by two agents from the well-known mouse network. Of course I'd heard of this group and their good works, as what mouse has not? But it was my first opportunity to see at close range the valiant endeavors they undertake all over the world to further the interests of our great community, so hard beset by cruel treatment by both humans and beasts. Their message was from a long-lost cousin I hardly knew I had, though he'd heard of me in his faraway region because of the sea adventures I'd undertaken with my friends Anton and Cecil."

"You had sea adventures together?" Montana asked.

"Oh yes," Hieronymus replied.

Cecil yawned and passed a paw over one ear. "Don't get him started on that story," he said.

"Right," said Anton. "Just stick to the tale about your cousin."

"Eponymus," Hieronymus said. "Sadly I've yet to meet him. But his message was that he was enjoying life in a distant clime and that he hoped I might join him there.

"I had been thinking of relocating for some time, as I had no family in the vicinity of our port, so I decided to undertake the journey. The messengers met me at the ship and showed me a safe mouse-entry hole. The sea journey was uneventful and when I arrived at a large port city, the network had sent two scouts to meet me and escort me, first to a very fine dinner and then to the landship, where they helped me to select the best carriage. For the first few days all went well. Other mice, some who had made the trip more than once, got on and off, advising me of what to expect along the way. They suggested the best places to stop over and have a meal, and they were very clear about the timetables of the landships, so I was never uncertain about my progress.

"At last we came to the town where my cousin lived. I asked around until I was directed to his house, where I was met by a most pleasant mother mouse with two children. She told me that Eponymus had learned there was a great ocean at the end of the train tracks, as well as a fine city where every mouse lived like a king. His longing for sea air had been too much for him, so he had decided to make the move. 'It's not much farther on,' this kindly mother assured me. 'Only two days on the landship, and you can't miss your stop because the track ends at the shore.'

"After resting for a day or two in this town, and rescuing the matron's babies from a very obnoxious bird who had it in mind to make a lunch of them, I decided to follow my cousin to the fine city.

"On the next train things went very wrong. There was a fire in my carriage and I escaped by running along the roof of the cars. But alas, I descended abruptly through an unexpected opening and dropped right into a carriage designated for human passengers. I was alarmed at first, but no one saw me and it was very nice in there, with lots of room and good smells. I ran along the wall under the seats and jumped into an open basket that was full of bread and cakes. I ate until I was full, not at all worried about missing my stop, as I knew everyone would get off. *This is the way to travel,* I thought. I could see why humans are so keen on it.

"Then I fell asleep and when I woke up a lady and a little girl were staring down at me. The lady was screaming. The little girl smiled and slammed the lid shut before I could get out, and I was trapped. I was in that basket for a long time and when at last the cover was lifted, a great black paw reached in and grabbed me before I could escape. It was a man's gloved hand and it dropped me into a cage.

"Naturally I began to plan my escape. Anton can tell you that I am not one to give up easily and I'm well versed on survival techniques, but this cage was a truly diabolical fabrication made entirely of metal with a latch I couldn't open no matter how I tried. I was given food and water, and there was a device that I used for exercise—a wheel that allowed me to run without ever getting

anywhere, which as you can imagine, is a very dis-
heartening way to pass one's time.

"After weeks of imprisonment, I thought of my
friends Anton and Cecil and I decided that my last
hope was to send a message to them through the
network, using the only two landmarks I could see
from the front and back windows of the house—the
whale and the coyote. It was the parrot Dayo, a
very intelligent though often difficult roommate,
who told me the human name for the fearsome
creature on the sign.

"And so I sent my message and waited. I had a
good deal of time to think about my life, my family, and my future, and I was in a great despond
to think I might end my days trapped in a cage at
the whim of humans. I could not fathom why they
would take pleasure in keeping a creature they
otherwise recoiled from in horror locked up in a
wire box in which they provided food, water, and
exercise, enough to keep me alive, but they would
not give me liberty. I had the feeling that something about my helplessness made them fond of
me, but how could that be? In this awful state,
near despair, I looked up at last to see my deliver-
ance in the form of my two friends' faces upside

down outside the window. I can't describe my joy at that moment, or the thrill of escape. And so I came to this place to spend a magical night in the company of cats, great and small. What a life I've had."

Here the mouse ended his story, gazing at his audience with warm confidence. Cecil had drifted off to sleep early on, but Anton and Montana had stayed awake, curious to hear Hieronymus's tale. In fact the Great Cat was wide-eyed and rapt with attention. Anton thought it was odd that such a powerful and solitary animal as Montana would be so fascinated by the story of a mouse's travels. But then it dawned on him: solitary—that was the word. Alone up here on his mountain Montana was free and never afraid. But there was no one to tell him a story. And that was sad.

Imagine, dear reader, if there was no one to tell you a good story?

Anton also observed that the mouse network was a lot more efficient and helpful if the traveler in their care was another mouse. They had met and assisted Hieronymus at every point along the way, recommending the best places to find meals and making sure he had comfortable accommodations.

Anton and Cecil had had to eat bugs and berries, take advice from dogs, and risk their lives careening around on hoofstock. Yet it appeared that everywhere Hieronymus went, he was welcomed by knowledgeable and helpful mice!

Anton smiled at Hieronymus and his attentive audience, the Great Cat. Cecil was snoring softly, and the only other sound was the mouse patiently answering a question Montana asked about his escape. Anton felt safe and strangely happy. For the first time since their journey began, he wasn't homesick. In the morning he and his brother would set out with their little friend for the ocean at the end of the track. He was sure Cecil would want to go on. If there was an ocean, there would be fish. Fresh fish. That would be all Cecil would need to know.

❖ ❖ ❖

A warm wind blew through the night, and the cats awoke to see tumbleweeds chasing one another down the alleyways between sheer faces of rock. Cecil felt dry down to his bones. He longed for the smell of sea air, the feel of the waves under a ship, the cool blue expanse. These mountains were interesting in their way, but too hard and dusty for a sea cat. So he was glad to hear that they would be journeying onward to another ocean, even if it meant more travel on trains.

Montana accompanied them as far as the edge of town and helped them find one last big meal to fill their bellies before they set off. The four creatures sat in the morning breeze for a while, enjoying the sunshine and cleaning their ears and whiskers with their paws, and then it was time to go.

"I wish you well," said the Great Cat, gazing at each of them in turn. "In some ways I'd like to see what you are seeking—a great ocean. Your story has shown me that there's much I don't know about the world. But I fear that a cat of my size might attract a lot of attention."

"It would be hard to hide you on the train, that's for sure," Cecil agreed.

"We can tell you about it when we come back through this way," said Anton.

Hieronymus gave his friend a look both pensive and doubtful, but said nothing.

Montana looked down at Hieronymus. "I do most humbly thank you, small mouse, for rescuing me from that trap. I might have died there, were it not for you." He bowed his head slightly.

Hieronymus flushed. "Happy to be of service," he said quietly.

The Great Cat nodded thoughtfully. "Cats are wild beasts no matter how much time they spend around humans. And we must watch out for one another, care for each other when we can. Anton and Cecil came to rescue you, Hieronymus, as you have rescued them and now me. That makes you one of us, I think. In addition to your many mouse relatives, we are your family as well. Be safe."

Montana lifted his great head and breathed in, catching a scent on the breeze, and then he bounded away toward the mountains. The cat brothers and their small mouse friend watched him go in silence. From beyond the hills far away to the east came a familiar pair of sounds—a high whistle and a low, rhythmic chugging—and they turned and hustled toward town to catch their train.

The train that pulled into the station trailed various types of carriages behind the engine, and the friends knew to choose an open box-like one and to avoid the many-windowed ones with people waving. Cecil allowed Hieronymus to climb on his back and hang on to his shaggy fur as the cats made the leap up into the carriage. The way the engine waited on the track, hulking and chuffing, reminded Cecil of Dirk and his bison friends, and he told Anton and Hieronymus that story while they rode.

For two days and nights they bumped and swayed along the track, the sights becoming stranger as they went. Steep climbs slowed the engine to a crawl and they wondered if it might stop altogether. Impossibly high bridges over deep gorges sent Anton scrambling to hide under the hay in their carriage until they were safely across. Cecil watched from the doorway one bright morning as the train approached a rocky mountainside without slowing, and one by one the carriages were swallowed up into a round black mouth in the rock until their own box was plunged into darkness and loud, echoing clacks were all they could hear. They huddled together, wondering what was to come, when the sunlight reappeared and the train continued on as it had, relentlessly rumbling down the track.

Cecil and Hieronymus became adept at dashing to find food during station stops—Cecil following his nose to a discarded meat pie or unattended leg of chicken, Hieronymus snatching a few berries or scattered grains, and once an entire wedge of cheese—while Anton stayed behind to sound the alarm if the train appeared to be leaving before the other two returned.

"Brothers! To me!" Anton howled from the station porch as the yard workers began closing the doors to the carriages. The three would dash to their box just in time and hide behind crates until the train began to move.

On the third day the train arrived at a big city with a bustling station to match, and when Cecil leaned out to check the ground ahead of the engine, he saw what they'd been waiting for.

"This is it, mates!" he said with a grin. "There's no more track past this station. We've arrived at the end."

"Can you see the sea?" asked Hieronymus anxiously.

Cecil looked again, stretching his neck, then working his nose. "I can smell it, for sure. Let's go!"

They walked to the roadbed where Cecil's nose led them and saw an inlet filled with sailing vessels and surrounded by busy dockside activity—but no wide ocean. Hieronymus drooped with disappointment.

"But where could it be?" he said, twisting his tail. "My cousin was sure there was a second sea here."

"You know," said Cecil, rubbing his ear with a paw. "The mouse network isn't so great on details. Maybe *this* is what they meant by sea."

"Oh, surely not," scoffed Hieronymus. He gazed around the inlet, frowning. "On the other hand, Cecil, you might be right."

Many people from the train, their bags and boxes in tow, had also made the trek down the road to this spot. They gathered along one pier as if waiting for something. At the far end of the inlet, a narrow waterway disappeared around a bend, and Cecil spied a type of vessel he'd never seen before emerging from there: a large, wide boat that seemed to move not with sails, but with huge wheels that churned and slapped at the water on each side. The boat approached the pier amid a great splashing mist.

"Will you look at that?" said Cecil. "It's like a cart, rolling on top of the water."

The churning slowed and stopped, and the wheel boat pulled even with the pier. Many humans disembarked down a steep ramp, after which the other waiting humans boarded and the ship pushed away. The cats watched as the wheels propelled it across the inlet and around the bend again.

"I have a feeling we should have gotten on that ship," said Hieronymus. "Perhaps it keeps going to the ocean."

"Let's wait and see if it comes back, like the fishing boats do," said Cecil. "In the meantime, this is the perfect occasion for a snack." He bounded happily down to the docks and soon returned with a crusty loaf of bread in his jaws for them to share. They tucked themselves between two buildings and dozed in the sunshine for a while, until Anton's ears pricked up.

"There's the sound again," he said. "The splashing of the wheel boat."

And sure enough, there it was, paddling across the inlet like a duck. This time the friends snuck aboard and hid under a tarp covering a dinghy on deck. The wheel boat set off and navigated a narrow band of water for half a day, arriving at a similar pier in an even bigger city than they had left. The most thrilling part was the view that opened before them as the boat docked and they emerged from the tarp.

"Oh, my whiskers!" gasped Hieronymus. "The story was true, after all."

A wide, blue ocean stretched all the way to the horizon, the crests of the waves lit by the setting sun. A pod of dolphins played in the distance. Great ships plied the waters, their sails raised, their flags snapping. The nearby harbor was filled with the masts of schooners, barques and brigs, clippers and sloops, and the shorebirds swooped and gamboled in the wind. Above it all floated a welcome aroma: the briny tang of fish. The familiar feel of home washed over the three friends as they stood on the deck for a long moment.

Then quick as a wink they slipped down the gangway and through the crowded streets until they arrived at a high cliff overlooking the shore and the sea beyond. They stood side by side, overwhelmed by the sight, grateful that they were together and in one piece after all that had happened.

Finally Hieronymus heaved a contented sigh. "In all my days," he said softly, "I've never seen the sun dipping *into* the ocean. Only rising out of it. We must be on the other side of the world."

"Is this sea as big as the other sea—*our* sea—do you think?" Anton asked, his gaze sweeping over the water.

"Nah, couldn't be," said Cecil, shaking his head. "Our sea is huge."

Hieronymus stroked his whiskers thoughtfully. "Does this sight make you two eager for more adventures?"

The brothers answered at the same time. "NO," said Anton. "YES," said Cecil.

Hieronymus chuckled. "That's what I thought you'd say."

"What about you?" asked Anton. "Now that you're free, will you go home again?" He sounded unabashedly hopeful.

"I'm getting on in mouse years, Anton. This may well be my last journey." The cat and mouse exchanged a glance, and a look of understanding passed between them.

Cecil was distracted by something on the beach below the cliff. "What in the name of the Great Cat is *that*?"

The other two peered over the edge, following his gaze. Rising slowly above the sand close to the cliff wall was a contraption so unlikely that it left their jaws slack. An enormous basket, of the kind that fishermen used to store their catch but many times larger, swung gently in midair, kept aloft by a giant swollen balloon. The basket had no lid and held a man who watched the bright blue balloon carefully, pulling on the various ropes that connected the basket to the balloon, and tending to a stove that sent up a great *whoosh* of fire. As the basket ascended Cecil could see inside, and to his surprise it was furnished with chairs and a table spread with a cloth and what looked like sandwiches on a plate. Very slowly, chuffing rhythmically, the whole assembly rose straight up in front of them. As it passed the man spotted them and waved.

"Amazing!" cried Cecil. "In the space of one day I've seen two astounding things—a wheel boat, and now this—a giant basket floating on air. I like this place!"

"I like that we're *together* in this place," added Anton.

Hieronymus smiled. "We're agreed, then. We'll try our fortunes on this end of the world for a bit." His black eyes gleamed and he grasped a pawful of fur on each brother.

But Cecil was gazing up at the big balloon as it caught the wind and bobbed landward. His eyes were wide and his heart throbbed with excitement.

"Cats in heaven, it's an airship," he said softly. "What a way to travel!"

ACKNOWLEDGMENTS

We want to thank our editor, Elise Howard, and our agent, Molly Friedrich, for their ongoing dedication to the cats. We're also grateful to the team at Algonquin Young Readers for their enthusiastic and tireless efforts to guide Anton and Cecil, as well as the humans who wrote about them, as they make their way in the wide world. Thanks especially to Eileen Lawrence, Emma Boyer, and Brooke Csuka for provisioning us with maps, supplies, and timetables for each new adventure, and to our meticulous copy editor, Dan Janeck, who lets nothing slip.